OK

**"YOU KNOW, THIS IS A SECRET FANTASY
OF SOME WOMEN," LISLE WHISPERED.
"TO BE CAPTURED BY A PIRATE AND
TAKEN TO A BEAUTIFUL DESERTED
ISLAND IN THE CARIBBEAN!"**

"Is it yours?" Hal murmured.

"No. Mine is the Viking fantasy." She laughed lightly. "Handsome. With graying hair along the temples. And strong, but gentle. Like you, Hal." She ran her fingers through his hair.

"You have a strange imagination, woman."

"Only because it gets me through the rough times."

"Your imagination?"

"My fantasies."

"Well, then I want to be a part of your fantasies," he said firmly.

"Oh, you are, Hal. You most definitely are," she assured him.

"But when are you going to take me seriously? When are you going to put me in your real world, where I belong? Where I want to be?"

CANDLELIGHT ECSTASY ROMANCES®

TWO SEPARATE LIVES

Tate McKenna

A CANDLELIGHT ECSTASY ROMANCE®

Published by
Dell Publishing Co., Inc.
1 Dag Hammarskjold Plaza
New York, New York 10017

ISBN: 0-440-18848-2

Printed in the United States of America

First printing—April 1985

In everyone's life,
There are times
When reality and fantasy interlace.
When change is imminent, and you look back
to see
how far you've come.
And you know
The best has just begun.

To Our Readers:

We have been delighted with your enthusiastic response to Candlelight Ecstasy Romances®, and we thank you for the interest you have shown in this exciting series.

In the upcoming months we will continue to present the distinctive sensuous love stories you have come to expect only from Ecstasy. We look forward to bringing you many more books from your favorite authors and also the very finest work from new authors of contemporary romantic fiction.

As always, we are striving to present the unique, absorbing love stories that you enjoy most—books that are more than ordinary romance. Your suggestions and comments are always welcome. Please write to us at the address below.

Sincerely,

The Editors
Candlelight Romances
1 Dag Hammarskjold Plaza
New York, New York 10017

CHAPTER ONE

Lisle Wheaton stuck her Tony Lama–booted foot on the wing of the airplane that would provide her escape. Her long legs, usually so strong and sure, faltered at the knees, and she gripped the handle beside the door with a shaky hand. *This fear of flying has to stop!* she told herself firmly. *Today. Here and now. It's just a short flight to the island. Close your eyes, and you'll be there soon.*

She glanced hesitantly at the pile of orange and white tin beneath her two-toned boots. These small commuter planes scared the hell out of her, no matter what she told herself. Inhaling deeply, Lisle straightened her curly-lamb vest and adjusted the leather belt that matched her expensive footwear, then bent over to crawl inside the twin-engine Cessna. A male voice, calling from below, caught her attention.

"Hey! Can we grab a ride?"

Lisle, bent into a most unladylike position with her rear in the air, straightened immediately. She cast an impassive glance over her shoulder, then proceeded to watch with growing interest as a slim, silver-haired man sprinted onto the runway of the small Maine airport. His russet leather sport jacket flapped open as he ran, and her eyes were drawn to his firm, trim waist. He moved with the smooth, easy flow of a jogger. His tan slacks couldn't hide the ridges of muscle across the tops of his thighs, and Lisle couldn't help admiring his superb form.

When he reached the tip of the plane's wing, he called,

"It's too late for another flight, and you're the last one out! We'd like to go along with you." He barely panted from the run while behind him a slightly overweight couple scurried to catch up with him.

Lisle shrugged, knowing the delay would prolong her agony, but she was grateful for it. "Better ask the pilot. I'm just a commuter."

"Well, tell him I'd like to speak to him, please. It's imperative that we catch this flight." Obviously he was accustomed to being in a position of authority, for he had taken charge almost instinctively. The other couple reached him, panting and wheezing, with luggage in tow. The man turned his attention to them while waiting for his directive to be acted upon.

Lisle secretly bit her lip to keep from mocking his assertive manner and commanding voice. Instead, she drawled sarcastically, "Sure thing, bud." Then she adjusted her gray felt Stetson with its ostrich-feather band, bent over again, and proceeded to slide her slim hips into the tight copilot's seat. "You're a popular guy today, Gene. There are three prospective customers under the wing."

The pilot sighed. "It always happens on Fridays. People miss the ferry and rush to get to the island for the weekend." He inclined his handsome head toward her. "These folks want to go to Grand Manan?"

With the proper jaunty hat Gene could be a younger version of Indiana Jones, an adventurer and a hero. Maybe he was just the one to help her overcome her fear of flying.

"I think so." Lisle smiled coyly, the impostor in her appreciating the young pilot's flirtations.

"Do you mind if they tag along? It will cost you less if you share the charter fee with them. Course, I still want you to sit copilot with me." He winked amiably.

Lisle smiled bravely, privately amused by his behavior, yet unwilling to foil the deception. She knew that Gene thought she was a younger woman. And yet a small devil inside her kept her quiet. Or maybe it was the woman in her. It felt good to be admired by a younger man, and although she would definitely keep this situation under control, Lisle could still enjoy it.

"I have only one question," she said seriously. "Will this plane hold all of us?" Lisle had visions of luggage being tossed out to lighten the load as the plane settled lower and lower over a wildly tumultuous ocean.

Gene frowned. "You aren't afraid, are you, sweetheart? Of course it can hold all of us. Anyway, don't worry about me ditching in the ocean. I can set this baby down anywhere. She takes to water as well as land."

"Oh. Good." Lisle, with a fixed smile, imagined them adrift somewhere in the vast North Atlantic with waves crashing against the windows of the plane. "That's a relief," she muttered. Her imagination was definitely running wild today.

"Don't you worry that pretty head of yours about a thing, sweetheart. Gene'll take good care of you!" His weathered hand patted her knee.

"I'm sure you will," she responded uneasily. "Well, you don't want to keep your prospective clients waiting."

"Gotcha. I'll be right back, so don't go away." Gene climbed out of the pilots' quarters and hopped down to greet the newcomers.

Lisle waited somewhat nervously. *Where would I go? This is my only way out! Like a fool, I missed the ferry and I'm stuck here, or believe me, I wouldn't stay two seconds!*

Gene talked to the tourists and then helped them load their luggage and get seated in the back of the airplane.

Lisle gave perfunctory nods but paid little heed when she was introduced to the passengers. During the bouncy six-mile flight from the Maine coast to the tiny island of Grand Manan, her attention was fixed on the complex instrument panel before her and the churning ocean below. She gave a

13

silent prayer: *Oh, God, let this handsome young pilot know what he is doing, and let the engines hold.*

Oblivious to Lisle's nervousness, Gene expounded on the rudiments of piloting a twin-engine Cessna. It was to his boastful testimony of his years of flying experience that Lisle clung, her smile concealing inner fears. *Damn!* She shouldn't have missed that ferry!

Gene, on the other hand, could only hail the rare opportunity before him and wasn't about to let it slip away without giving it his best effort. It wasn't often, on this lonely Maine-coast charter run, that he got a chance to meet a real Texan. Yet here she was!—a gorgeous woman in tight jeans, high-heeled boots made of some kind of snakeskin, and authentic cowboy hat, and with a sweet, sexy drawl. He would be stupid not to make the most of the occasion. She had to return to the mainland in a week, didn't she? Maybe then they could become better acquainted. Perhaps they could spend some time in Boston. She was a damn good-looking woman!

Soon they sighted the craggy coast of Grand Manan, a little jade jewel in the midst of the tumultuous blue-gray ocean. Lisle gasped in amazement at the rugged beauty. Oh, how she loved the little island. Several times over the past few years Lisle had made the pilgrimage to this remote northern Atlantic haven, although she had always traveled by the safe ferry route. To Lisle, it was almost like a trip back in time, providing a chance to escape her busy world. This time though, escape seemed even more urgent. Here was the one place where she could relax and forget.

"Well, what'll it be? By land or by sea?"

"W—what?" Lisle snapped her eyes away from the churning ocean.

"I told you I could land us on the water! Do you want a little excitement?" He asked the question loudly for the benefit of the passengers in the rear, apparently hoping they would opt for the watery landing.

14

"NO!" Lisle exclaimed, then lowered her voice to continue in a calmer tone: "No, thank you, Gene! The land. Please land on the land!" Only after the words were out did she realize what she'd said and how ridiculous she must have sounded. However, clear thinking was difficult for her at this point. The island was in sight, it was only minutes away. Why didn't he just get them there?

"Land on the land, the lady says!" Gene chuckled and then smoothly eased the plane onto a tiny gravel landing strip.

Lisle could hardly wait to set her feet on solid earth and breathe the salty air. Wasting no time, she squeezed out of the seat and stepped onto the wing, inhaling deeply, gratefully. Fresh air was above her! And the blessed earth was beneath her feet! Before she could hop down, the silver-haired man raised his hand to help her down. Now, Lisle wasn't helpless, but this was quite a jump, and she felt a little weak-kneed after the jostling ride. Automatically she reached for his strong, warm hand and alighted with the secure assistance he offered.

As soon as her feet touched the runway a stiff ocean breeze whipped under the brim of her hat and blew it away. Immediately the man who had helped her down hurried after it.

Gene, a suitcase in each hand, halted beside Lisle. His eyes assessed her completely, as a man will do, traveling from her rich, wind-tossed hair to her booted toes and back again. His expression registered astonishment, even admiration.

She's still damn good-looking, he thought appreciatively, *for a woman of her age!* In a low, rather sheepish voice he muttered, "You must have been laughing all the way over here. Why didn't you tell me?"

I couldn't. Don't you understand that I needed your compliments? Every woman does sometimes. . . . Lisle submitted her most justifiable smile but refused to apologize.

"Please believe I wasn't laughing at you, Gene. I was too busy worrying about flying. But you're such a smooth pilot, I've abandoned my plan to return by ferry. I'll fly back with you."

Gene hoisted the suitcases. "The next time a gorgeous dame gives me the eye, I'll look under her hat first. You're the smooth one, not me!" He wheeled away from the attractive woman who was old enough to be his mother.

"But I didn't give you the eye—" Lisle's hand went instinctively to her hair, shoving her stylish silver streak behind one ear. It wasn't tucked completely out of sight but merely flowed more gracefully through her mass of dark hair.

"Your *chapeau* . . ."

Lisle turned, a little flushed from the pilot's rebuff, to face the man who held her hat. "Why, thank you. You've certainly gotten your exercise today. First, to catch the plane. Now, to retrieve my hat. I should have known better than to wear it up here with all this wind." Lisle gazed up into the bluest, most penetrating eyes she had ever seen. Silver hair framed his distinguished face, a straight nose crossed angles with his clean-shaven chiseled jaw, and his mouth was a pair of tapered, but not-too-thin lips.

The man was tall and lean with an aura of polish that hinted of vast experience. She sensed that his eyes—they were the intense royal blue of the North Sea—had seen war and famine, good and evil. They could appreciate love and beauty, for life had taught him to take gratification where he could. She imagined him dressed as a Viking warrior, in a leather kilt with metal vest and helmet, the sun glinting on the blade of his spear. She closed her eyes against the sharp glare.

"It was no trouble at all. Gives me a chance to introduce myself again. I'm Hal Kammerman. Sorry, I didn't catch your name on the plane."

Her eyes popped open, and Lisle shifted a step to the left.

16

Back to reality! Muffling an embarrassed chuckle, she managed a terse "I'm Lisle Wheaton." His gaze washed over her like a hot shower, dispersing a warm glow through her body, from head to toe. For a moment she felt young again. . . .

"Where are you staying on the island?"

"The Lighthouse Inn. I was lucky to get a room this late in the season. And you?" She took back her hat and edged it through restless fingers.

Hal noticed that there was no wedding ring on her slender hand, and that her tapered nails were manicured. "I'm staying in a friend's cottage. It's just over that hill from the inn. Is this your first visit to Grand Manan?"

"No," she answered softly. Quickly, perhaps too quickly, she was beginning to feel that his questions were invading her privacy. This is what she came to the island to avoid. The questions. The invariable friendliness. The male pursuer. "I've been here several times. Lovely this time of year, isn't it?"

Hal's blue eyes crinkled when he smiled, and he warmed to Lisle in spite of her coolness. "I've been here several times over the years too. Strange that we've never met."

"Yes, I suppose."

"Texas, huh?" he said musingly, trying to draw her out. "That's quite a distance from here."

She smiled and quipped, "How did you guess?"

He shrugged, and she admired his broad angular shoulders as they shifted inside his leather jacket. "Well, there's your sweet southern drawl, curly-haired vest, snakeskin boots, cowboy hat, and armadillo belt buckle. Otherwise, you could be from anywhere in the country!"

She laughed aloud. "You're right. I guess I do emit Texas today."

His questions persisted. "Which city in Texas?"

"Dallas."

Dallas. Hal felt a pang of mixed emotions, of remembrances of times past when he had visited Dallas and an-

17

other beautiful woman. A woman in love with another man. Kathryn. She probably still lived there, with her husband and child. Hal found it too painful to stay in touch, but she had sent a birth announcement a few years ago.

Spontaneously he said, "I have an old friend in Dallas. Kathryn Coleman. Do you know her? She's married to a senator."

"I've heard of Senator Coleman. Big ex-football player?"

"Yes, that's the one. I haven't seen her—seen them in several years." The distant expression in his eyes vanished just as quickly as it had appeared. "Actually, I would have guessed you were from Dallas. Or maybe Houston."

"Oh?" She turned to lift a bag from the plane.

"Sure. You look so cosmopolitan." With hard-muscled arms Hal easily swung his luggage down, then fell into step with her to follow the other passengers to the station wagon that waited to take them to their island lodgings.

"You just told me how western I looked with my boots and hat," she complained. "Now you say I'm cosmopolitan?"

"You have a classy look. And you wear this western stuff well."

"Thank you." She looked down and studied her footsteps on the gravel road.

"Lisle, are you alone? Or are you meeting someone here?"

She halted and looked up into his deep royal-blue eyes. This man was obviously interested in her and wanted to strike up an acquaintance. Well, maybe a brief friendship wouldn't be so bad, but that was as far as it would go. Brief and friendly. Her life had been too complicated recently for her to want another involvement.

"No, I'm alone." Perhaps she should have told him that she was meeting an old love. Or that she had no interest in getting to know another man. But was that how she felt about this Viking of a man?

18

He grinned. "Good," he said honestly. "Then maybe we can see each other again while we're here."

"Maybe." Neither of them had made any promises.

"I know this sounds trite. Or maybe nosy. Or both. But why does a beautiful woman like you come to a place like this alone?"

"You're right. It's both trite and nosy."

"Sorry. But you're so attractive, I'm sure you have men clamoring over you."

Lisle smiled tightly. If he only knew! "Now you're sounding even more like a cliché. 'What's a woman like you doing in a place like this?' is an old line."

"The line is *'attractive* woman like you,'" he noted calmly. "But you still haven't answered my question."

Lisle hesitated. "What about you? Why are you here alone?"

"It's a good escape. I came here once with my wife. After her death several years ago, I found I missed the special qualities the island offers. The peace and quiet. So occasionally I come back."

"I'm here to escape too," Lisle said softly, then mentally finished the brief admission: *To escape the clamoring; the eager men; the constant questions; the pressure cooker of work; the demands of family; the recent embarrassment; the media.*

"To escape?" he said, determined to coax a better answer out of her. "That's something you usually hear from men who want to get away from their stressful jobs. You must be a corporate executive. Or maybe you run an oil company in Dallas."

"No." She laughed, shaking her head. After that there were a few minutes of silence until he spoke again.

"Well, are you going to tell me what you do? Or do I have to squeeze that out of you too?"

"I . . ." Lisle's voice broke. Here she was, caught in the very trap she was trying to escape. The interested men. The

19

never-ending questions. Next would come the clamoring. Her voice seemed to answer on its own: "I'm hardly an executive. Actually, my job is very dull. I, uh—I'm in retail sales. Women's clothes. Very dull stuff, and I'm extremely low on the totem pole."

He smiled gently. "I'm not surprised you work in the fashion industry. You look so stylish. Even I can tell you're wearing designer jeans."

"Oh, I get a discount on this off-the-rack stuff," she hurried to explain, flicking an imaginary hair from the lambskin vest. "You know how some people can throw some sale items together and make it all look expensive. Actually"—she leaned toward him with a gleam in her eye—"I'm a company mushroom."

"A mushroom?" Hal realized the minute he repeated the word that it was a joke.

"Yeah." Lisle grinned impishly. "They keep me in the dark and feed me just enough manure to keep me quiet."

"Oh, I asked for that one." Hal laughed heartily as they approached the station wagon.

Lisle handed her luggage to the driver, privately pleased that she had halted the questions and perhaps cooled Hal's interest. Couldn't he tell that she didn't want to get involved? Truthfully, until she had started talking, Lisle hadn't even been aware of how strongly she felt about this escape business. She hadn't intended to lie about her job; she had just wanted to steer the conversation away from it. She didn't want to think about it, talk about it, or answer the million questions that invariably came with the admission. She wanted freedom. Relaxation. Escape. And she only had a week to enjoy it all. And anyway, she had told only a half lie.

She could hear Hal instructing the driver to deliver his luggage to the inn. He then turned to Lisle. "Meeting you certainly has been a pleasure, but I hope you don't mind if I walk from here. I spent most of today sitting and could use the exercise. Maybe we can get together later."

"Sure, Hal." Lisle smiled at the Viking and watched him turn away. Then she faced the couple who were already seated in the station wagon, and started to climb in beside them. But something intangible pulled her back. On impulse she tossed her heavy felt cowboy hat on the seat and told the driver to leave her things at the inn. She gave him a tip, then started after Hal. It was like the half lie. She didn't know why in hell she did it. "Hal? Would you like some company? I haven't had much exercise today either, and I need to stretch my legs."

Surprised, he glanced over his shoulder and said, "Love it." He smiled. "Can you make it that far? Two miles?"

"Sure." Lisle stuffed her hands into her jeans pockets and rocked back on her heels. She hauled in a deep, lung-cleansing breath and started walking at a fast clip. "Ah, this air is so clean and pure. And cool! I love it."

Lisle repressed the primitive urge to run with arms outstretched to embrace this beautiful little island-world. She was free for a week! No one here cared that her face graced the covers of popular magazines. There were no photographers lurking nearby. Nor were there demands from anyone. She was alone with a Viking hero, who knew the ravages of war. She chuckled privately as her imagination began to churn again.

The station wagon drove away, leaving the sound of the Cessna's engine in its stead. Lisle turned to watch the commuter plane's takeoff.

"I'm afraid I embarrassed the pilot," she admitted sheepishly.

"Oh? You mean on the trip over here?" Hal had watched the little male-female interchange that took place in the cockpit during the short flight to the island. With the cowboy hat covering the gray streak in her hair and shading her face, Lisle had the appearance of a much younger woman. He could certainly understand the young pilot's mistake.

"Well, he . . . thought I was much younger and . . ."

Hal grinned. "And you didn't discourage him."

"Neither did I encourage him," she hurried to explain. "He offered to give me a lesson if I sat in the copilot's seat. I just agreed." She shrugged innocently, yet the sophistication expressed in her face denied innocence.

He took broad steps to catch up with her fast pace. "I have to speak in the young pilot's defense. You are a very attractive woman, Lisle."

"Oh, come on," she returned modestly, embarrassed by his flattery. "You don't have to patch up my bruised ego!"

"I was just stating a fact."

"Remind me to get your number so I can have my ego reinflated periodically."

"It would be my pleasure, I can assure you."

They walked in silence for a few minutes, absorbing the peace of the remote island. Occasionally the crash of waves against the shore and the lonely cry of a sea gull could be heard.

"You're a jogger, aren't you?" Lisle asked, her wild imagination picturing the Viking in running shorts and little else.

"Yes. I wish I could run today, but it's impossible to jog in Top-Siders." He spoke in a gently mocking tone as he kicked at a small pebble in the road. "I should have changed shoes."

"Well, take them off and jog barefooted. You don't have to wait for me. I don't mind walking alone."

"Are you a jogger, too?"

She shook her head. "I do jazzercise, three or four times a week."

"Jazzercise?"

"It's like aerobic dancing."

"Then you should be in pretty good shape. Take off your boots and run with me."

With violet eyes sparkling, she smiled at the thought of herself behaving so impulsively. "Go barefooted?"

"It was your suggestion," he returned. "Maybe if we both took our shoes off, we wouldn't look so peculiar."

"You want company in your craziness, huh?"

Her eyes danced with laughter, reminding Hal of flowers in the wind. "Why not?" He shrugged. "It's more fun to be crazy together."

Lisle bent to remove her left boot. "Why not! If you're game, I am!"

In a matter of moments they were jogging along, laughing, barefooted . . . young again. Hal stuffed his Top-Siders into his back pockets and tucked one of Lisle's heavy boots under his arm; she carried the other one. Neither gave a second thought about how odd they looked. They were following an impulse, together in their craziness! It was fun to unwind and relax, and it seemed perfectly natural that they should seek their lost youth on this remote island.

In a remarkably short period of time they had managed to break away from their separate worlds to enter into an enchanting escapade. To watch them, one would think that placing both feet on the soil of Grand Manan Island was an act of magic. And indeed Lisle and Hal were transformed.

A tired but laughing couple with graying hair and faces that spoke of experience wobbled up to the porch of the old house that now served as a country inn. After mopping their dripping brows and helping each other into shoes and boots, Lisle and Hal gathered their individual luggage and panted a spirited *"Hasta luego"* . . . until later.

Lisle waved and watched her imaginary Viking disappear over the hill, a suitcase clutched in each hand. Then she dragged her feet up the steps of the Lighthouse Inn.

She renewed her old acquaintance with the feisty innkeeper, Mrs. Pinksten, who was known to all as Pinky. Undoubtedly the nickname derived from her surname, but Lisle secretly thought it referred to the pink-tinted nose of this

23

wiry little lady, for she seemed always to be getting over a cold and dabbing at her pinched nose with a tissue.

Pinky insisted on carrying the heavier bag and led the way down the hall. The wood floors creaked with every step. Lisle trudged along behind, carrying her small makeup case. The cross-country trip ending with the two-mile jog had definitely taken its toll.

She stepped inside her favorite room with a tired but appreciative smile. Located at the back of the house, the room had large dormer windows that looked out on the distant lighthouse.

Pinky, slight of build and always energetic, scuddled about the room, adjusting the curtains, turning down the bed, making sure everything was just so. Patting Lisle's arm, she said, "Have a pleasant stay, dearie. Dinner is at six," and then hurried away.

Lisle knew that meant if she wasn't at the table on time, she would miss dinner. She smiled now as she looked at the familiar surroundings: the chintz wallpaper with its tiny blue flowers, the ornate antique furniture, the brass bed covered with an intricately crafted quilt. *Old. Pleasant. Comfortable. Relaxing.*

She crossed to one of the windows and raised it a few inches. Cool, salty air rushed in, and Lisle breathed in the strong but satisfying odor of brine. A dominant fishy smell wafted into the room, but it was expected and tolerated. The aroma of smoked herring was just a part of the ambience of Grand Manan. With the window open Lisle could hear waves slapping against the rocky shore and the occasional blare of a foghorn. Away at last. Now she could relax. She could already feel the tension begin to slide from her body.

Leaving the window slightly opened, Lisle began to unpack. For someone who spent most of her waking hours displaying the most beautiful garments in the world, the assortment of clothes she had brought along was certainly motley. She pulled out thick cable-knit fisherman's sweaters

24

with patched elbows and stretched necklines, heavy argyle socks that reached to her knees, plaid scarfs for protection against the wind, and faded denim jeans. There were no designer labels in sight.

Purely from habit, Lisle hurried through her task, neatly folding things and placing them into dresser drawers. Then abruptly she stopped and looked around. What was the big rush? She had already arrived. Here on her perfect island there was no need to push, for there were no deadlines to meet. Nothing but dinner at six. She could relax. Slow down. Enjoy.

Eagerly Lisle discarded her heavy cowboy boots. She grabbed her favorite gray-and-purple argyles, sat on the edge of the bed, and began to pull them on. Then she stretched out on the multicolored quilt coverlet. Listening to the waves lapping against the shore, Lisle felt herself relaxing . . . and drifting.

At a quarter to six, in time for Pinky's dinner hour, Lisle emerged from her chintz-decorated room looking totally different from the chic woman who had earlier flirted with a handsome young pilot and jogged with a dashing Viking.

Her feet were cozy in the argyle socks and a very comfortable pair of thick-soled suede walking shoes. She had changed into a pair of gray cotton cords, which were unfashionably baggy. Her bulky ultramarine cable-knit sweater had seen better days. All in all, Lisle was extremely comfortable, though her look was somewhat sloppy. But it suited her fine, and she slouched gratefully inside the soft garments.

The guests were gathering for the evening meal, some introducing themselves, others renewing old acquaintances. Before Lisle had a chance to join them, Pinky breezed in from the kitchen, a steaming bowl of clam chowder in her hands. "Seems you have a visitor, dearie," she said with a knowing smile. "He's out front, waiting for you."

"Thank you, Pinky," Lisle murmured, and peeked through the front window. She caught sight of Hal Kammerman and hurried out to greet him, suddenly feeling like a young coed on her way to greet a visiting suitor.

Hal leaned against a tandem bike, his feet crossed at the ankles, his arms folded casually across his chest. He looked marvelous in his white canvas pants and light-blue pirate shirt. An argyle sweater was tied loosely around his broad shoulders. Her heart skipped a beat when she saw the argyle. *Aha! A man of my own taste!*

Smiling, she said, "Hi. I didn't expect to see you so soon."

He shrugged. "Frankly, I didn't expect to be here so soon either. But I got myself invited to a neighborhood beach party and thought you might like to come along. Sorry about the short notice, but my cottage doesn't have a phone."

"What's this . . . contraption?" She pointed to the bike. "Looks like something from my great-aunt Agatha's day."

"This, my dear, is a bicycle built for two. It is a relic from your aunt Agatha's day, but it's the local version of a taxi. Best I could do at this time of evening. This place isn't exactly a bustling metropolis, you know. So, what do you say? Care to come along for some steamed clams?"

"Well, I don't know. It's time for dinner at the inn," Lisle mumbled, motioning toward the house.

"To hell with dinner at the inn. Come with me. It'll be much more fun. You didn't come up here to follow a time schedule, did you? Be spontaneous!"

Her violet eyes flickered. He was right! It would be great fun to be spontaneous. Then she remembered what she looked like. "I really should change clothes."

"You're fine just the way you are," he insisted. "No one will care what you wear. Everyone is casual here. And I promise not to tell them you sell ladies' wear."

Lisle flinched at his words. Why in the world had she told him that she sold ladies' wear? Well, she would have to continue the charade. And dressed this way, she would not be recognized. "You're very convincing, Hal. Sounds great."

"I would advise you to grab a jacket. It gets pretty chilly on the beach at night."

Within minutes Lisle and Hal were pedaling, in tandem, across the small island, laughter bubbling around them. The romantic bike ride heightened the merry mood and Lisle's sense of a restored youthfulness. Maybe a little innocent fun with Hal the Viking wouldn't be a bad idea, after all.

There were only two other couples at the beach party, and Lisle could see right away why Hal had invited her. One lone single at a party of couples was no fun.

Norman and Irma Palmer, the pudgy couple from the commuter flight, had come all the way from Fort Wayne, Indiana. It was their first trip to the Northeast, or anywhere beyond a hundred-mile radius of home. They owned a hardware store. Lisle decided that since she barely knew screwdrivers from pliers, she would be hard-pressed to find anything to say to them.

The other couple, Madge and Bill Arthur, hailed from Boston and ran a travel agency. Ah, that was more like it. At least they would have traveling in common. As Lisle shook hands the first words out of Madge's mouth were "Don't I know you from somewhere, Lisle? You look so familiar."

Lisle ducked her face into the flickering shadows of the campfire. "No, I don't think so. I've never been to Boston."

"Oh, it could have been anywhere, we travel so much. Well, maybe I'll think of it. Is this your first trip to Grand Manan?"

Praying that Madge would go curl up behind a rock on the beach, Lisle answered, "No. This is my fourth trip here."

"We've never been here before," Irma chimed in. "Boy, that smell of smoked fish gets to you after a while, doesn't it?"

"You'll get used to it." Madge dismissed Irma's comment

27

and turned back to Lisle. "All the way from Texas, huh? Tell me, do they still have those horrible dust storms?"

"Oh, it isn't so bad now. Better soil conservation has helped." Lisle looked at Hal, a strange expression on her face. The questions were starting. Oh, God, was there no end? Damn! Maybe she should have lied about her hometown too. Everyone seemed to have a million questions about Texas. Suddenly she felt very vulnerable.

Although he didn't understand what was wrong with her, Hal felt obliged to bail her out. "Here we go, gang," he called, lifting the cooler lid. "We have beer and white wine. What'll it be?"

They all placed their orders and gathered around the campfire. It crackled invitingly, and Hal and Lisle sat together on a blanket he had brought.

"Lisle, we don't have to stay here long."

His eyes were understanding and reassuring. Surely he could sense her discomfort, but he couldn't know why she was upset. Somehow, though, he gave her strength, and she smiled and took a grateful sip of wine.

"I'm fine," she said. "The fire is wonderful and warm. Isn't it a beautiful night?"

Hal popped the top of a Stroh's and motioned toward the sky. "Clouds moving in. Could mean rain. We'd better enjoy it while we can." He settled beside her on the blanket and pulled the argyle sweater over his shirt.

Even in the growing darkness Lisle could tell how absolutely masculine he looked in the sweater. She longed to run her hand along the diamond designs and feel his muscular chest beneath the knit. Then she flushed, and was grateful for the concealing shadows. After all, she hardly knew this man!

The others moved closer and began to talk about their careers. Inevitably the questioning turned to Lisle. "And what do you do way down there in Texas?"

Lisle cleared her throat and spoke with a nervous laugh.

"I'm in women's wear retail." There, that sounded innocuous enough.

"Does that mean you sell ladies' clothes?" someone asked.

"Yeah. Something like that." Quickly she pointed the conversation away from herself. "What about you, Hal? What do you do?"

"I'm a management consultant. I go around the country analyzing companies' problems and telling them how to run their businesses."

"Fascinating," commented Madge.

"Wonder if he could help us with any of our problems?" Irma said, nudging her husband.

"Oh, Irma." Norman spoke reprovingly. "We don't have any problems."

"Oh, yes, we do. What about the bad debts we can't collect?"

"Excuse me." Hal spoke to the group, but specifically for the Palmers' benefit. "But I only deal with large companies. They hire me for an evaluation and consultation."

"Well, I'm going to evaluate these clams, folks." Bill pushed aside some of the glowing embers and began to dish out the piping-hot crescent shells.

Darkening shadows engulfed them, and Lisle and Hal huddled together on the blanket, seeking an elusive warmth. He had another beer; she accepted a second glass of wine; and they fed each other clams dipped in melted butter.

For some reason Norman had decided that extra light was needed, and now produced a brilliant battery-run invention that bathed their entire section of beach in an unnatural light. It was the newest item in stock at his hardware store back home. The light completely destroyed the romantic shadowy ambience, but no one had the heart to tell him. So they just sat in the glare, staring at one another for a few moments.

Abruptly Madge's voice pierced the night, her comments terminating Lisle's well-played charade. "I know where I've

29

seen you!" she shrieked excitedly. "I've seen your picture in a magazine. I'm sure of it. You're a model, aren't you? I know I've seen you in some of those women's magazines!"

"Yeah, that's right!" Bill Arthur hit his knee with his hand. "And I saw your interview in *Playboy!*"

"*Playboy?*" the other couple chorused, leaning forward with renewed interest.

For a moment Lisle considered flatly denying it all, but she was already boxed in by her own doing. One look into Hal's curious eyes and she wanted to confess. And explain. "Well . . ." She began hesitantly, hoping he would understand.

But Madge, her eyes aglow, interrupted before Lisle could go any further. "I read where you're one of the highest paid 'older models' around! Actually Bill pointed out the article in *that* magazine, or I never would have seen it. How did it feel to be in *Playboy* magazine?" She leaned forward in eager anticipation.

"I . . . well, it was similar to being interviewed in any other magazine." That wasn't exactly the truth, but Lisle wanted to de-emphasize her exposure in the girlie magazine. It had been an advertising ploy, but who in this gathering would believe that?

Her secret was out, and she was mortified that she had lied about herself. Maybe it would have been better just to take it on the chin at the beginning. No, damn it! She was here to get away from the incessant questioning and the unpleasant clamoring. Lisle tightened by the minute as their questions became a barrage. And it was the same old barrage she had heard hundreds of times.

"How did you get into modeling?"

"I modeled for a friend's small dress shop, and a modeling agency spotted me."

"How long have you been modeling?"

"Off and on for about twenty years, but steadily for the last eight."

"What do your children think of your occupation? Did they see the *Playboy* article?"

"My children are adults, and they're proud of my business."

"You have *grand*children, don't you?"

"Yes, two."

"Do you dye your hair? Did you bleach that streak?"

"NO!" Lisle could feel the resentment and anger swelling inside her, threatening to explode.

Still the questions continued. "Do you get your clothes free?"

"NO! Nothing's free! Please . . . I . . ." The wall she had built around herself had crumbled to the ground, and Lisle felt tired and vulnerable. She wanted only to escape. Struggling to her feet, she turned to Hal. "This night air has given me a chill. I'd like to go back to the inn."

"Sure, Lisle." Hal was on his feet, folding the blanket. His voice was uncommonly soft, his expression pensive.

Lisle managed polite thank-yous to her hosts and new acquaintances but privately vowed that she would not allow herself to be trapped in their company again. She certainly didn't need this! Not on vacation! She and Hal mounted the bicycle built for two and rode the mile and a half back in complete silence. Suddenly the vehicle wasn't so romantic when you had to stare at someone's back and wonder what he was thinking. By the time they reached the inn, though, Lisle had ceased to give a damn what Hal thought.

The porch light glowed yellow, and Lisle again felt herself a coed, now returning from a date. "Hal, thanks for inviting me tonight. I honestly didn't intend for all this to happen."

His cold blue eyes assessed her. "Obviously. Is that why you lied to me? Did you also pose in the nude for *Playboy*? Is that what made you one of the highest paid models?"

"Hal! I thought you, of all people, would understand! But I see I was badly mistaken!"

"I was mistaken too! I thought you were a lady! Now I

31

find I don't know a thing about you! What's the truth, Lisle?"

"A lady!" She smirked. "What era is this—1910? So what are you going to do about your besmirched reputation, Mr. Kammerman? Tar and feather me and turn me over to the townsfolk? Actually, they couldn't be much worse than those piranhas tonight." She mounted the porch steps two at a time and slammed the door behind her. Tears of anger and frustration swam in her violet eyes. How she regretted the furious comments she had just flung at Hal. Damn! She had screwed everything up—royally!

CHAPTER TWO

Lisle was aroused to semiconsciousness by the noises. Thunk-thunk . . . thunk. She fought to remain asleep, lulled by the whine of the wind. Then the regular knocking. Tap-tap . . . tap. *Regular knocking? The door! Someone's at the door! Who could it be, at this hour? What the hell time is it, anyway?*

She struggled to a sitting position and clicked on the bedside lamp. But there was no light. Click-click, again. Nothing. *No electricity?*

The knocking continued. "Lisle? Are you all right?"

The masculine voice was vaguely familiar. But who could it be? She scrambled around in the dark, groping for her robe, running her hand hastily through her hair. She reached for the doorknob, then froze. What in hell was she doing? Opening her door to a strange man in the middle of the night?

"Who is it?" she demanded, suddenly wide-awake. "And what do you want?" She listened with pounding heart.

"Lisle? Are you all right in there?" This time it was a woman's voice. "I'm just checking on everyone, dearie. It's Pinky."

"Oh, Pinky." Feeling a little foolish, Lisle threw open the door. The warm yellow glow of burning candles now illuminated the room, and she saw that it was Hal who stood behind Pinky. Lisle stiffened immediately.

"And Hal Kammerman came along," Pinky said unneces-

33

sarily as she fluttered past Lisle, moving around the room while she talked. "Hal was concerned about you, and so was I. Didn't mean to wake you, dearie, but I could hear this shutter flapping in the wind and wanted to check your windows. Any leaks in here? Now, please stay away from the windows. You never know when a tree will come crashing down in a storm like this." She patted Lisle's arm and then scurried away to check on her other guests.

Lisle folded her arms and grated, "You were concerned about *me?* The woman who lied to you and proved *not* to be a lady?"

Hal loomed before her in the glow of the candle he held, a disheveled vision of strength and authority. His unruly hair curled around his head, a few frosted strands glistening in the golden light. The deep blue eyes swept over her in a sharp and all-consuming scrutiny. "I came to apologize."

"A-apologize? You? Why, I thought I was the one who'd sullied your reputation with my lies and wanton ways!" She motioned dramatically toward her heart.

His chin jutted proudly. "Are you going to accept this apology gracefully, or will I have to force it on you? I've thought about that party all evening, Lisle. They were pretty rough on you. So was I. I threw you to the wolves and then didn't even give you a chance to explain."

Her violet eyes softened at his words, and after a moment's hesitation she said, "I do owe you an explanation, Hal. And I feel guilty as hell about lying. As lies have a way of doing, they just kept growing. And, not having much experience with twisting the truth, I didn't handle it well." The wind whined more piercingly, and Lisle pulled her robe tighter. The deep burgundy velour garment hugged her skin intimately, nestling snugly in a V-shape against her neck and breasts.

Hal swallowed heavily, suddenly jealous of that damned robe caressing her smooth skin. "Could we talk about it while the storm rages outside?"

34

"If you want to." She nodded toward the love seat with its comfortable chintz-covered pillows.

"We really shouldn't be so close to these windows. Help me pull it out in the hall. That way we'll be protected in case something crashes through." Hal placed the candle on a shelf in the hallway and then rested a small brown bag against a cushion before grabbing the end of the sofa.

Lisle heaved the other end. Nodding toward the oblong bag, she asked, "What's that?"

He grimaced with the final tug on the heavy piece of antique furniture. "There! They don't make love seats this sturdy anymore." From the bag Hal pulled a bottle of white wine and began a worthy discourse, complete with appropriate antics. "This, my dear lady, is Canadian white Riesling produced in Canada's Great Lakes region. It has a distinctive perfume, a touch of sweetness, and is perfect for a party in a storm, and for getting acquainted. Or reacquainted, as the case may be. It'll help keep us warm while the wind howls outside."

In spite of the angry words they had exchanged only a few hours before, Lisle had to smile at Hal's performance. The Viking had a sense of humor as well as a temper. "And it's laced with truth serum, I presume?"

He shrugged and turned his head to the side. "Ummm, perhaps it will function as such for m'lady."

"To show you what a good sport I am, I'll get the corkscrew and a couple of glasses," Lisle said amiably, and started down the hall toward the kitchen.

"Wait up!" Hal called, and slid a broad hand into his pocket, pulling the material tight against his taut, muscular thighs. Smiling triumphantly, he produced the all-important item. "Even in my haste to escape my leaky roof and the rising tide, I did think of the two most important things to salvage in an emergency. The *vino* and a corkscrew! There is nothing worse than a tampered-with cork, or those tiny broken-off pieces that float around on the surface of your wine."

35

He made a face, then inserted the tip of the instrument into the cork and began to twist it.

She laughed. "I like your sense of priorities. Now, we still need glasses, unless you thought to bring those along too."

"No, the wine and corkscrew were all I could manage while riding single on a tandem bicycle in a forty-mile-an-hour wind. I was just lucky I beat the rain."

Laughing gaily, she shook her head as she imagined Hal battling the raging elements to reach the inn. "I admire your courage, sir. I'll be right back with the glasses." She lit another candle, and made her way to the kitchen.

When she returned, Hal filled their glasses and proposed a toast. "Here's to our own private storm party. And a budding friendship."

"And the whole truth," Lisle added, and tipped her glass against his. "Is that my cue to clarify the situation and clear my good name?"

"As you wish, m'lady."

They settled comfortably on the sofa and sipped the delicious wine. The occasional rumble of thunder or bolt of lightning reminded them that a storm raged outside while they sat warm and dry in the hall of the Lighthouse Inn.

"I'll start," Lisle offered. "Old friends in Boston introduced me to Grand Manan Island over eight years ago. It—it was a private haven for me after my husband died."

"And now you come back each year for renewal?"

"I can't get back every year because of my hectic schedule. But whenever I come here, I feel that I'm making a complete escape. Life moves at a slower pace, and the pleasures are simple. I like that. I can wear old jeans and a torn sweater, and nobody cares. There are no photographers or reporters looking for a scoop."

"That's why you didn't want to be recognized?"

She took a deep breath. "This year has been particularly stressful, both at work and in my personal life. As we approached the island something came over me that demanded total anonymity. I needed to escape completely for the brief time that I was here. Meeting you complicated the issue, Hal, but still I was reluctant to reveal all. You saw what happened at the party. People go crazy and think they can ask you anything and everything. They forget you are a real person who needs some degree of privacy. It's happened to me before, and I just wanted to avoid it this time."

Hal spread his hands apologetically. "And here I am, plying you with questions about all those private details of your life again."

She smiled gently. "I don't mind. Honestly. I wanted to explain to you. And apologize."

"And I wanted to apologize to you," he said, using the back of his hand to caress her cheek. "For putting you in such a vulnerable position and not being more sensitive to you. I could tell something was wrong, but just wasn't wise enough to put it all together. By the end of the evening I was feeling . . . left out. There were things I didn't know about you, and perhaps I felt I should know those things. I was beginning to think I, too, was like the proverbial company mushroom!"

She laughed with him. "Sorry. That was my fault."

"And, I must admit, I find it hard to believe you're a grandmother."

She shook her head ruefully. "They're still babies, but I'm a lousy grandmother, Hal. My grandchildren don't have the usual cookie-baking, always-available granny. I'm too busy to baby-sit. And I never seem to be around when the really important things happen. I do make an effort at birthdays and holidays. Thanksgiving is my big day. Once a year I bake pumpkin pies and roast a turkey."

He lifted her hand and stroked its long soft fingers, the polished nails. "These gorgeous hands make pumpkin pies?"

"I make a scrumptious pie," she informed him, only mildly indignant. "In my former life, as housewife and mother, I was an excellent cook."

"Frozen or from scratch?" he asked doubtfully.

"From scratch, of course!" She extended her glass for more. "This is very good wine. As was your idea to share it. I don't even mind your waking me up."

He refilled their glasses. "I have only one question. It doesn't really matter, mind you, but I'm just curious."

"Yes?"

"Did you really pose for *Playboy?*"

"No! Of course not!" She scoffed. "I did consent to an interview. Which, incidentally, was the idea of my publicity manager, who arranged it all. It was for publicity, believe me. The magazine then ran some of my layout shots to accompany the article. The most risqué among them showed me in a floor-length nightgown with my entire leg revealed by a slit up to the thigh."

"Not bad, I'd say." Hal smiled admiringly.

"What?"

"A grandmother with legs good enough to be shown in *Playboy!*"

"That's not exactly what my son said, but he recovered quickly." She laughed. "And what about you, Hal? Do you have children? Or grandchildren?"

Hal shook his head. "My wife and I had only one child. He was stillborn. Beth could never get pregnant again. She died ten years ago."

The conversation turned mellow. Apologies had been offered and accepted. Truths had been revealed. An easy ambience was established between them. Lulled by the unaccustomed wine and the late hour, Lisle scooted lower and lower on the small sofa. Murmuring something about the comfort of remaining warm and dry indoors while a storm was raging outside, she nodded her head against Hal's outstretched arm.

Lisle fell asleep first, slumping comfortably on Hal's firm shoulder.

He wrapped his hand protectively around Lisle's shoulder

and pulled her against him. He felt her slow, regular breathing and imagined holding her, making love to her. God, how, suddenly, he wanted her! It was crazy! To feel such strong desire for a woman he'd met not more than twelve hours ago!

And yet these feelings for Lisle seemed to go beyond masculine lust. He had been so disturbed after the party that he had been unable to sleep, even before the storm hit. Guiltily Hal realized he had exposed her to the caprices of the public and allowed them to pick her apart.

He looked at her face, now relaxed in sleep. Her dark lashes brushed her high cheekbones, and finely etched lines spread fanlike at the corner of each eye. Her skin, though, was flawless, and her generous mouth and slender neck retained their classic lines.

Besides her obvious beauty, her intelligence and wit were apparent to Hal. Here was a smart, active woman to whom he could relate, and whom he enjoyed being around. Oh, yes, he could find great pleasure in pampering her . . . and in loving her. *God!* Hal thought brusquely. Whatever made him think of that?

Finally Hal slept, too, although his was an unsatisfying, fitful sleep.

At dawn the storm blew out to sea, leaving debris scattered across the tiny fog-shrouded island of Grand Manan and two people bundled together, dreaming dreams of love.

Lisle and Hal spent the week as a twosome, exploring the small island as if they'd never been there before, seeing everything there was to see. They found new joy in climbing around the lighthouse and hiking to North Head to watch the fishing boats come and go. They rented a car to tour the entire island and found a well-hidden cove where they made a delightful picnic of smoked herring and Irish potato bread. Often, after walking the pebbly beaches, they stayed to

39

watch the tremendously high tides roll in to cover the rocks and mist the air with sea spray.

One particularly foggy day Lisle and Hal lunched in a small restaurant near the wharf. Gulls screeched incessantly overhead and the distant foghorn kept up a steady blast, but the diners' youthful spirits couldn't be dampened.

"Do you like this dulse?" Hal nibbled politely on the crispy island specialty.

"That dried seaweed stuff?" Lisle wrinkled her nose. "It's horrendous! I'd have to be starving!"

"You have to acquire a taste for it." He spoke in a maddeningly reassuring tone.

"You actually like it?" She gasped.

His blue eyes tried to mask his deception—he had in fact repeated a line from a travel brochure—but eventually he broke into laughter and grabbed a piece of bread. "Horrible! I'd have to be starving too! But this dish you'll love." He motioned to the deep-dish pie the waitress set before them. "Moose-meat pie."

"M-moose?" Lisle wrinkled her nose again and began poking at the savory dish. "Where's the moose?"

"You won't find moose meat in it. There's potato, apple, and breast of goose."

"Breast of what? No moose? Do you mean there's actually no moose in moose-meat pie?" Lisle feigned astonishment. "Then why do they call it moose-meat pie?"

"My dear," Hal said patiently, "do you actually think anyone would eat something called goose-meat pie?"

She nodded with a twinkling smile. "Those who eat dulse!"

The lunch was typical of their time together, filled with laughter and pure enjoyment. Later, as they walked a rocky stretch of the eastern beach, their conversation became serious. "I want to make love to you, Lisle," Hal said softly.

"Hal, I'm fifty-one years old."

"I don't care if you're a hundred and one! I want you! Want to make love to you. Just think about it, Lisle."

"Oh, I'm thinking!" Lisle grabbed at a piece of grass that brushed her jeans as she trudged along the rugged beach. "Aren't we too old for this kind of . . . fooling around?"

"Too old for sex?" Hal stuffed his hands deep inside the pockets of his trousers, stretching the denim tight against his thighs. He pondered for a moment, then replied with a twitch of a smile, "Fifty-three isn't too old to fool around. Why is fifty-one?"

"Hal, be serious. This isn't something to take so lightly." Lisle sighed, and her face was tight with the mixed feelings that tore at her.

She refused to look at him for fear her cold exterior would melt to reveal a warm inner soul that might consider an affair with the right man. *The right man!* Was Hal the right man for her? Who could know after only a few days? But he seemed so right. Handsome. Intelligent. Interesting. Sexy. A Viking hero in a fisherman's sweater and jeans. But she pulled herself up short. *It's too soon! I just can't go through this again.*

"Believe me, I'm trying to understand." Hal followed Lisle's long strides, staring at her squared shoulders and ramrod-straight back. "Maybe there are some things I don't understand about women, Lisle. Do you stop fantasizing about love? Does age destroy that wonderful ability?"

"Of course not!" Lisle's eyes twinkled. "I have a very active imagination, filled with dreams of love and caring."

"Then why the hesitation?"

"You're asking me to have an affair with someone I met only a few days ago. We barely know each other, Hal. Give me time."

"Lisle, listen to me." Grasping her forearms between two firm hands, he turned her around to face him. She looked into those striking blue eyes of his and could feel the melting process taking place inside her. "It's been a wonderful week.

41

We have to go back tomorrow. I admire you, Lisle. A lot. I think the feelings are mutual. Forget about the major decisions of having an affair. Let's spend the evening together and enjoy. If it leads to making love, then so be it."

"You make it all sound so easy."

"It *is* easy."

Her chin snapped up. "Well, I'm not! I can't—"

"Sorry, Lisle." His voice became gentle. "I shouldn't have said it that way. You're a very special lady. One I want to get to know better. Our time together is so limited now. I'm a man with a strong desire—for you, Lisle. Is it so wrong to want you completely?"

His eyes chilled her. His straight nose, the jutting chin, the wind ruffling through his silvery hair, all worked together in her mind to create an image of the strong Viking.

"No, I guess it's—"

"Normal! It's perfectly normal." He gripped her arms even tighter before releasing them.

"Yes, I suppose so," she whispered as he turned away to stare out to sea. He was frustrated with her, she could tell. "Hal, I'm not as free as you are," she explained. "I have a family to think about. And my career." Why did she always bring them up at times like this? Men didn't want to hear about careers and children. Or grandchildren, for God's sake!

Lisle plopped down near a clump of sea oats and dug her boots into the pebbly shore. The sea gulls circling overhead cried into the ceaseless wind. In the distance a foghorn sounded. The ocean extended as far as the eye could see. They were in as remote a place as they could possibly be.

"Why must you think of your children at a time like this? Do they have to be a part of this decision?" Hal sat beside her on the beach and clamped his arms around widespread knees. "Children, this is Hal," he said mockingly. "We're thinking of spending the night together. Just a brief encounter, you understand. Should we or shouldn't we?"

42

Lisle cast him a stern glance but said nothing. He still would not be serious.

"Lisle, this is just between us, two consenting adults."

She rested her head against his sturdy shoulder. "Perhaps someday, Hal. Right now is too soon for me."

His strong arm curled around her and his hand squeezed her arm. "Someday is now. Don't throw away this moment for someday. Lisle, you've been married. Surely you miss that intimacy with a man?"

"Of course I miss it. But I don't like flings. And that's exactly what this would be. We're parting tomorrow. I just don't want this kind of brief affair, Hal."

"Have you had them before?"

"Affairs?" She clasped his hand firmly, gaining strength from the contact. "There have been a couple of lovers since my husband's death. I—I've just had a very unpleasant experience with a man, Hal, and I hope you understand why I'm not eager to try again so soon. It has nothing to do with you. It's my problem."

"Which then becomes mine. I really don't care about the other men in your life, Lisle. I want to know how you feel about me. Aren't you attracted to me, Lisle, as I am to you?" His finger traced the outline of her chin and tilted it up for a delicate kiss. The coming together of pliant lips, smooth velvet to smooth velvet, ignited sparks of long-dormant desire. Neither of them could break the binding propulsion and end the electric sensations of the kiss. Not just yet, anyway. In a natural motion Hal's fingers stroked her arched neck and traveled down to cup one of her small, rounded breasts.

Lisle's response to his touch was immediate, and she gasped softly as his fingers pressed into her. His kiss deepened, opening her lips to further sensations. Her nipples grew taut under his gentle caresses, and she ached to feel his hand warm against her flesh. Oh, yes, she missed this kind of intimacy with a man. Missed the warmth, the companionship, the love. . . .

When their lips finally separated, Lisle was subdued—she had indeed melted a little more inside. In a hushed tone she revealed carefully hidden emotions. "That should tell you how I feel about you. I'm very much a romantic, and you have captured my imagination. In a way, Hal, you're a real-life version of the man of my dreams, my fantasies. Here, in this remote place, you're my blue-eyed Viking, ready to capture me and fling me over your shoulder! What I really want to do is forget my inhibitions and run away with you. We could laugh together and enjoy each other and make mad, passionate love!" She recoiled from his touch, amazed that she would say such things to him. "Have I shocked you?" she asked in a small voice.

A strange expression crossed Hal's chiseled face as he examined her anew. "No, I'm not shocked. Surprised, maybe. Relieved that you can tell me these things. A Viking, huh?"

She grinned impishly. "I can imagine you standing on a far ledge overlooking the ocean and your rugged island domain. You would be wearing a sheeps-wool loincloth and a bearskin flung over your shoulders!"

He threw his head back and laughed, a long and deep laugh. "Well, I don't have much experience as a Viking, but if I dared to capture this lovely damsel, first thing I'd do is toss the loincloth aside and wrap our bare skin together in my bearskin blanket!"

"Somehow I knew you'd say that." She smiled warmly, her violet eyes dancing.

Hal shifted and pulled her to him, pressing her back to his chest. His arm curled around her slender waist. "We were meant to be together. Can't you see? We've already run away, Lisle. We are the Viking and his woman. Grand Manan is our fantasy island, our retreat from the world. We don't have to think about our families or friends. It can be only for this night, if that's what you want. This one wonderful night. Just the two of us, all alone, enjoying fun and fantasy and renewal of lost dreams." He gestured at the broad expanse of ocean before them. "We're all alone and free."

"Please, Hal, you know I'm weak." She toyed with his wrist, slipping two fingers inside his sweater cuff to feel his pulse. It was nice to have Hal's arms around her, to rest against his chest. To be captured by a Viking.

"Good. Then you can be as weak-kneed and smitten as I was the minute I saw you. Still am at the thought of having you in my arms."

"Smitten?" Lisle laughed and turned in the circle of his arms to face him. She traced his lips with a warm finger. "What an old-fashioned word. *Smitten. . . .*"

"I'm an old-fashioned man." He lowered his lips to hers. His kiss, no longer gentle velvet, had become a strong cord of passion wrapping her tightly in its force. The pressure of his mouth against hers ignited the ancient yearnings of a woman for a man, and Lisle opened her lips, allowing his tongue entry.

Spirals of desire spun through her, and she pressed her softness to his hard warmth, touching her tongue to his. This intimate mingling of their bodies—first the meeting of lips, then the invasion of his sweet satin tongue—kindled a soaring blaze inside her. There was only one way to put out the fire, and they both knew it.

Finally Hal raised his head and murmured, "Now, is that old-fashioned?"

"Hmmmm, ancient. But I love it." She smiled happily. "I think I'm smitten by you, Hal Kammerman. I'm old-fashioned too."

"Thank God," he murmured. "There's nothing worse than being smitten alone." His silken kisses trailed down her slender neck.

"Hal, I do want you. Surely you can tell that," Lisle muttered softly, and framed his face with her hands. She looked

45

hard into his blue eyes. "I want you to make love to me, and to return the pleasure myself. But I'm a woman with a family, responsibilities, and a demanding career back home. I never intended for this little interlude between us to last longer than this week."

"We'll love for today and let tomorrow take care of itself."

She shook her head. "No. I can't do that."

"So, you're saying that when we leave this little fantasy island, our affair that was never fully consummated will be over."

She sighed. "Oh, Hal . . ."

He kissed her again and moved to cradle her against his lean form. He lifted his head and muttered gruffly, "Fair warning, m'lady! The Viking doesn't let his woman go easily. I will require a lock of hair for your freedom!"

He tugged gently on the silver streak in her sable mane, bringing her close to him—so close that she quivered in response to the energy surging through his body. Lisle could feel against her thigh the hard ridge of his aroused passion, and she wanted to urge him closer still, to the part of her that was aching for intimacy with him. A woman needed a man, even a fifty-one-year-old woman. Sometimes a woman needed a love affair. And love. Was a woman ever too old for warmth and affection from a man? *The right man!*

The sudden cooling of the ocean breezes fanned the heated emotions of the couple locked in an embrace on the rocky shore. "Keep me warm," said Lisle encouragingly as she shivered against Hal's body.

"Let's go to the Viking's lair, woman," he rumbled. "It's too cold to stay here on the beach. We'll light a fire and have some grog and . . . whatever Vikings eat. Maybe a little of yesterday's Brunswick stew?"

"Yes . . . sounds nice." She laughed at his musings. He had to be disappointed in her. Maybe even hurt. Yet he continued to joke. He still wanted her near. Hal Kammerman was quite a man. He made her feel young and wanted. And,

46

yes, even sexy. Was that so bad for a woman of fifty-one? No, she decided quickly. It was extraordinary, something to be cherished. And she admitted to feeling a certain inflation of her sagging self-esteem when Hal talked eagerly of desiring her. It made her feel eager for him too.

He pulled her up. "Shall I heave you over my shoulder for the full effect?"

"Would it spoil the effect if the Viking's woman came willingly?" She slid her hand into his.

"Not as long as you realize that you're captured and can't escape."

She smiled up at him as a breeze swirled around them, binding them into one figure. Hand in hand Lisle and Hal retraced their steps along the rocky beach, the wind ruffling their graying hair. But at that moment they were ageless— their dreamy eyes filled with youthful fantasies—as they entered Hal's empty cottage. It was silent there, and now they were indeed alone.

Lisle watched as Hal bent to light a fire in the black cast-iron stove. His back was strong and muscular; his masculine physique lean and attractive. There was a time when Lisle would have gone eagerly into his arms and willingly accepted his flattering offer of love.

However, that was before Kaplan. Now that she had made an absolute fool of herself, Lisle was reluctant to try love again. Next time she became involved with a man, there would be no expectations, no hopes for the future. No thoughts of love. Fortunately, Hal expected nothing more of her than whatever this week held. Or so he said. He wouldn't interfere with her life beyond this week. Or her family. Surely she could handle that kind of relationship. They would part as friends.

Lisle closed a window that had been left open to let in a few rays of the early-afternoon sun. Now, as the sun dropped beyond the horizon, the incoming air was chilly. Soon it would be dark. And then?

She slammed the shutters closed. The world would never know about their rendezvous. They were so far from the "real world"—on a little island so remote, it could be their secret forever. Maybe they would even meet again. Here. Next summer on Grand Manan. Then again, maybe not.

Hal stood back from the heater, hands on his hips, surveying the reluctant fire. He bent again, with his elbows propped on his knees, and blew lightly into the heart of the nest of sticks and papers. The unsteady flame immediately brightened.

"Aha!" he exclaimed with satisfaction. "There! That should warm up the place. Soon it'll be more comfortable in here." Hal rubbed his hands together in a gesture of accomplishment. Or maybe it was to hide his tenseness. Was it possible that he could be a little uptight?

"Nice fire," Lisle mumbled, suddenly tongue-tied and feeling extremely foolish because of it.

For a moment they stood facing each other in awkward silence. Lisle smiled apprehensively.

Hal smiled in return, a tight, forced smile. "What happened to the bold Viking and his fiery captured woman? How the hell can I uphold my fearless image if you play the shy maiden who's defeated before the battle begins?" He glared at her, his blue eyes flashing, his hands on his hips.

"Should I fight you off? Go down kicking and screaming?"

"Maybe. Is that what you want? A Viking who seizes a woman for his own wanton pleasure?"

"No." She smiled.

"Me either." Hal gazed at her for a moment, then his eyes softened. His expression told her he understood. Was it possible that she had found a Viking who cared about feelings?

Clearing the space between them, he took her icy hands in his, warming them in his firm, reassuring clasp. "Lisle, my dear little fantasy maker, there is no need to be wary of me. Or of our relationship. I'm not the forceful Viking of your fantasy. Seeking pleasure for us both is more my style. I won't force you into anything you don't want. Ever. Remember that."

Her voice was soft and raspy. "I appreciate you more than you'll ever know, Hal. You're exactly what I needed this week. A man to lift my spirits."

He lifted her fingers to his lips and kissed each one with pliable velvet lips. "A good-friend type? That's not what I wanted to hear, Lisle. If you dare say I'm a real gentleman, I'll bite your knuckles. I'd much rather be remembered as the savage Viking who couldn't control his lust."

"You're a savage beast," she said accommodatingly. Grinning, she touched his lips with her fingertips.

"I take that as a compliment." He kissed her lightly, allowing his lips to play on hers with soft, sensual touches. Velvet to velvet. His finger trailed down her cheek, then onto the sensitive skin of her neck. "Why don't you get comfortable on the sofa, and I'll pour some grog to warm our insides."

He tucked her under a heavy hand-crocheted afghan and returned shortly with two glasses of pale amber liquid. "Blended Canadian whiskey. Sure to warm the coldest heart."

"Did the Vikings sip blended Canadian whiskey? I thought they had grog."

"Well, then, blended Canadian grog!"

Lisle wrinkled her nose. "Blended grog has lots of calories! Don't you have any white wine?"

"Sorry, no white wine in the lair. You shouldn't have to worry about calories, with a figure like yours."

"It's my business to worry about calories. And I can't afford to ruin it in one little holiday."

"One little holiday? I was hoping this one would be memorable, not little."

She smiled softly, and her eyes glistened in the evening haze. "Oh, yes, Hal. I'll remember it for a long time."

49

"Right up there with the Grand Canyon and Disney World?" He raised his glass to hers. "Here's to a memorable holiday on a fantasy island with Lisle."

"And to the Viking."

"Hear! Hear! To the Viking! And bearskins!"

"Especially bearskins." She smiled and clinked her glass against his. *Our little fantasy island,* she mused. *Nothing lasting. Just for this week.* Those had been her words, her promise to Hal. Her protection for her own feelings. Yet, deep down, Lisle longed for love. Real love. Was it too late to hope for that? No! Without hopes and dreams, there was no future. Even now, she couldn't help wondering about a future with Hal. But those were dangerous thoughts.

"Hmmm, if the Vikings didn't have blended whiskey, they missed a wonderfully smooth drink." Hal stretched his arm around Lisle's shoulder. "I also put some Brunswick stew on the stove to warm. Surely the Vikings had that!"

"Or something similar. I think it was popular to put everything in one pot in those days."

"You know, even covered up with that blanket, you're a very sensual woman." He kissed her, sharing the flavor of blended whiskey that lingered on his lips. "And beautiful."

She returned his kiss, her teeth teasing his lips with light nibbles. "Isn't it time for that Brunswick stew?"

"Spoilsport," he teased affectionately.

"Hal, you said there would be no undue expectations tonight. No obligations."

He narrowed his blue eyes. "When did I say that? It must have been before I kissed you and became drunk on your—"

"Please spare me your *Romeo and Juliet* speech!" she interrupted laughingly. "Could we just have a bowl of hot stew now? Quietly?"

"So you can go back to the inn? Quietly?"

She nodded with unmistakable seriousness. "Yes, Hal."

Their magical week of fantasy and fun was over all too soon. Lisle had never felt so in tune with anyone as she did with Hal. She could privately admit that she and her late husband hadn't enjoyed each other the way she and Hal did —they had been too busy with kids and life's problems. And certainly she hadn't felt the same with Kaplan!

What she and Hal shared was a perfect fantasy! They had spent the entire week pleasing each other, doing all the things they wanted to, together every minute. They had laughed and talked at great length, communicating feelings and desires. It was fun and enjoyable and exciting. They had created something better than fantasy—something that was almost perfection. Almost.

Now as they stood waiting for the chartered plane that would return them to the mainland, they realized somberly that it was over: The fun and fantasy were gone. Lisle toyed nervously with an ugly red plaid scarf that persisted in blowing off her carefully coiffed hair. She retied it half a dozen times, grateful that it gave her fingers something to do, yet aggravated by the repeated annoyance.

Hal watched her until finally, in frustration, he snapped, "Why don't you just leave that damn thing alone. You look fine just the way you are."

"The wind is ruining my hair!"

"My God, Lisle, nothing could ruin your hair. Or you. You're perfect!" His blue eyes caught her in a penetrating look that quickly softened to a gentle caress. "I'm . . . sorry, Lisle. I—I'm just tense. This is torture for me. Could we . . . meet again soon? Surely you know I can't let you go completely."

She abandoned her hair to the vicious wind. "You want to see me again? Even though—though we didn't . . ."

He turned his face into the wind. "Yes."

"How about next year, same time?"

His blue eyes turned to cold ice. "No! Not good enough. A year is a lifetime away."

A grating noise announced the arrival of the plane, and they moved forward to enter the small craft. Gene, the pilot who had flirted with Lisle on the initial trip, was less friendly today. But she didn't care. She readily relinquished her copilot's seat to be in the back with Hal.

Their hands pressed together tightly. They said very little on the short flight to the mainland. For the first time in her life Lisle's thoughts during a plane journey were not focused on the hazards of flying. She was preoccupied with Hal and the look of agony that veiled his face. And she herself could not shake the feeling of absolute and total misery at the inevitability of leaving him.

As the plane began to descend at the Maine airport, Lisle murmured, "It's been wonderful, Hal." Suddenly she felt near tears.

His voice was a near growl. "I hate to see it end. So soon. And for so long. A year is too long for me to wait to see you again, Lisle."

She knew he was right. A year was too long for her to wait too. Her next words came spontaneously. "Then what about next month? I have to be in New Hampshire for an autumn style show and photography session in the mountains. Sunapee Lodge. The twenty-fifth. It would be perfect for a rendezvous." Having spoken, Lisle couldn't believe that those words had come from her own mouth.

Hal gazed at her solemnly, for a long moment. "Lisle . . . do you mean it?"

"If you can't make it, I'll understand," she whispered.

"I'll be there, Lisle."

With a kiss of lingering velvet lips and a tight squeeze of cold, nervous hands, they parted. The fantasy was over. They would return to their separate lives—lives that seemed worlds apart. The Viking was now the businessman in a three-piece suit, headed for Wilmington, Delaware, his lady-captive the stylish model, on her way to Dallas, Texas.

As Lisle's plane took off for Texas she closed her eyes to

force back the tears. She refused to ask herself what had happened between her and Hal. She only knew that it was the most wonderful time she had spent with a man in years. Instinctively she prayed that by the admission she wasn't setting herself up to be hurt again. Why had she told Hal about New Hampshire? Deep inside she knew why. She couldn't let it end either. Not yet, anyway.

Lisle told herself protectively that he might not show up in New Hampshire. And she would understand. However, Lisle's mind echoed with Hal's rumbled promise: *I'll be there.* She clung to those words, praying that her dream to see Hal again would come true.

CHAPTER THREE

"Mother! Are you home?" A polite knock preceded and followed the eager shout.

Lisle quickly finished pulling the leg warmers over her slim calves and called, "Be right down, Inga! Come on in."

Inga stood in the arboretum when her mother arrived.

"Liss!" a small child cried happily, flinging his chubby little arms around her neck. He was followed by his mother, a younger, blond version of Lisle.

Lisle remembered that when her children had broached the subject of what the grandchildren would call her, she had been quite angry at them for making her a grandmother. In her rebellion at the suggestion that the little ones call her Granny, Lisle had grumbled, "Let them call me Lisle. That's my name!" Liss was all young Alex could manage.

"Hello, you two!" Lisle embraced mother and son, then immediately began her apology. "As you can see, I'm on my way to exercise class."

Inga shrugged indifferently, although Lisle knew the spontaneous visit meant that her daughter was lonely. "That's okay," Inga said lightly. "We just stopped by for a minute to see how your trip was."

The questions came suddenly to Lisle's mind: Should she tell Inga about Hal? Could she even? And would it be fair? Inga, for all her striking good looks, didn't even have a current boyfriend. For some reason she just couldn't seem to meet the right man. So how could Lisle boast of a new man in her life? Actually, she might never see Hal again, so perhaps it was even premature to mention him. Anyway, after her disillusioning experience with Kaplan, both her children had become aggravatingly protective of her. No, she would wait a while before telling them about this new man.

"Liss, do you have a cookie?" Alex tugged on her leg warmer.

"No cookies, Alex. But I have carrot sticks. And yogurt pops."

Alex made a face. "No, thanks."

Lisle looked at her daughter admonishingly. "Inga, you really should improve his eating habits."

"Please, Mother. No lectures on nutrition. Grand Manan, remember?"

"Grand Manan was beautiful, as usual," Lisle began. "Oh, it was typical for this time of year. Cool. Windy. Unpredictable weather. We had a storm the first night I was there. It shut off the electricity and blew the shutters around a bit. Added a little excitement. Fortunately, by the next day it was gone."

Excitement, intrigue . . . romance. Lisle was now thinking of how the storm had brought her and Hal together. Actually, in the days following the storm they had barely parted. Ah, what a wonderful week!

"And did you get your fill of seafood?"

"Ah, yes! Lobster, fish, and lots of smoked herring. I still haven't learned to eat their awful dried seaweed, dulse, but the Brunswick stew was delicious. I ate so much, I probably gained ten pounds."

"You?" Inga scoffed. "You've never gained a pound in your life!"

"Oh, but I could, if I didn't watch myself carefully. And exercise. Which reminds me . . ." Lisle shifted uncomfortably.

"Yes, yes, I know. You're busy and we're going to be on our way. I'm just glad you had a good trip and are back

55

home safely. Don't forget Alex's school is having its fall festival in three weeks. Alex will be in his first play! He's going to be a tree! It will be precious!" Inga whisked Alex to the door. "We want you to be there."

"No, dear. I won't forget. So good to see you both. Let's get together later this week for dinner. Good-bye, Alex!" As she watched them leave, Lisle suddenly realized that she would, in fact, have to miss her grandson's first play. In three weeks she would be away for an assignment in New Hampshire where they would be showing new fall designs. There would also be a session for a fall photo layout for a national magazine.

The models would be wearing Safari lingerie, a line of wild jungle-print designs. Lisle had seen a few samples, and it was absolutely crazy. Leopard nightgowns. Zebra and snakeskin hose. Lion's-head bikinis, with real fur!

She grabbed a jacket, thinking how cold it would be in New Hampshire. She hoped the hardwood trees would be in full color. Maybe the maple trees would be ready for tapping.

But what mattered most was her promise to meet Hal in New Hampshire.

The plane gained altitude, plunging with shuddering force through the thick layer of gray clouds over Texas. Dallas would soon be experiencing an early-autumn storm. Bitter cold. Strong winds. Perhaps a coating of ice. The plane trembled again, and Lisle squeezed her eyes closed. Thoughts of iced wings and wind shears raced through her mind, and she said a quick prayer. *Not yet, God. There is still so much to do!*

"Lisle, are you all right?"

She opened her eyes to the anxious face of her friend, Andrea Haley. Lisle had fought for Andrea when she had applied for a job at Image International, the modeling agency. Andrea was a striking black woman, five ten with

56

gorgeous long legs, prominent cheekbones, and a complexion of the richest mahogany. She was proud, and it showed when she moved across a stage. Her only fault, if you could call it that, had been her age. Thirty-nine. Lisle had insisted that Andrea's maturity was an asset. Now, two years later, at forty-one Andrea was one of the most sought-after models at the agency.

Mustering a weak smile, Lisle tried to sound calm. "Oh, yes, Andrea. I'm fine. Just a little nervous with this rough takeoff."

Andrea patted Lisle's white-knuckled hand which was gripping the armrest between them. "When are you going to overcome this fear of flying, Lisle?"

"When I don't have to fly anymore," Lisle murmured sarcastically, then qualified her problem: "What I have is a fear of flying in storms." She refused to give in to the fear and continued to fly whenever her job demanded it. There was always the lurking dread that if she stopped, she might never fly again, and it was an important part of her business. Flying was like the dieting. Like it or leave the business.

"What you should do, Lisle," Andrea explained, "is close your eyes and think of something pleasant, like walking on a nice, sunny beach or . . . meeting this Hal."

Lisle closed her eyes and followed Andrea's directions. Her fantasy Viking stood on a cliff. The wind was ruffling his hair as it had the last time they'd been together. Lisle approached, and he turned and took her in his arms, his muscular thighs hard against her, his lips plying hers with tenderness.

Oh, dear God! Here she was dreaming about this man—this mature, silver-haired man—as if she were a young girl! He was a fantasy lover, someone with whom she had had a brief fling while on vacation. Nothing more. She would probably never see Hal again, even though she had told him about New Hampshire, and he had agreed to a rendezvous there.

She must face the possibility that Hal might not be there. It was too much to expect that he would be! She might as well forget the notion of another tryst with Hal. And forget him! But she couldn't. Hal Kammerman dominated her memory—this handsome man who had brought brief happiness to her lonely life.

Actually, her life was full in many important ways. Her two children and their families were healthy and relatively happy. She had darling grandchildren, good friends, a satisfactory career. She was even financially secure now. However, she lacked a close relationship with a man. True, it was something she could live without, as she had done for some time now. But, admittedly, she did miss it. The experience with Kaplan had been terribly disappointing. It had left her ashamed and unwilling to take such an emotional gamble again. She had vowed not to be fooled again and was reluctant to risk herself even with someone like Hal. But he provided everything missing from her life. Fun. Fantasy. Intimacy. Caring. At least, he *seemed* to care.

No, she couldn't—wouldn't—dismiss their time together. It was a fling, yes. But a wonderful fling. And if she never saw him again, Lisle would remember their brief encounter with a smile—and with no regrets.

She offered another silent prayer, this one a poignant plea: *Oh, please, send him to me again. Just once more.* The rattle of food carts interrupted her reverie and reassured her that they were flying steadily above the storm clouds.

To the polite request from the hostess, she gave the rote answer, "Coffee, please. Black. No peanuts, thank you." She sighed. Such was a model's fare.

"It must have worked." Andrea grinned at her seatmate. "We're now flying high, you made it safely through the turbulence, and you wore the nicest smile the whole time. Care to tell me about it? Were you thinking of Hal?"

"Of course," Lisle admitted readily. Andrea was her friend and confidante, someone who could understand. "He

58

makes a wonderful fantasy. Kind of reminds me of a Viking. Nice straight features."

Andrea's eyebrows shot up. "Viking? The brute type?"

"Oh, no, nothing like that," Lisle said with a chuckle. "Just his appearance. He's very athletic and . . . handsome."

"Sexy?" Andrea's dark eyes glowed.

After a moment's hesitation Lisle nodded. "Yes, I suppose you could say that. Although he's—he'd kill me for saying this—a real gentleman."

"Does that mean there's been no hanky-panky?"

Lisle's violet eyes lifted to meet Andrea's in a look of honest regret. "No. There's been no hanky-panky. I—I just couldn't handle another affair so soon after what happened with Kaplan. But I would like to see Hal again. Oh, Andrea, am I a fool? What if he doesn't show up in New Hampshire?"

"If he doesn't show, you've lost nothing," Andrea said. "But frankly, I don't think you have a thing to worry about, honey. If he's got any brains at all, he'll be there. And when he does show, you treat him right!"

New Hampshire was as Lisle had expected. Cold. Windy. On the verge of winter. And although she'd steeled herself against the possibility, she was still disappointed when Hal didn't show up.

For three days Lisle, Andrea, and four other models posed in the brief jungle-print lingerie, with broad smiles plastered on their faces as they frolicked about in the fallen autumn leaves pretending to be carefree and warm.

The last shots were done only hours before the group was to catch its plane, so there was a rush to take hot showers and prepare for the journey back.

"Thank God this assignment is complete." Lisle emerged from a steamy bathroom, wrapped in a hotel towel, her freshly washed hair still dripping. "I'm freezing! This is one time I won't have any qualms about flying back to Dallas.

Give me the warm sunshine of Texas!" She grabbed a turtle-neck sweater and scrambled into it.

Andrea, already dressed for travel, stuffed a last bit of clothing into her travel bag. "Don't be in such a hurry to leave, honey. There's a message for you at the front desk. I told you he'd come."

"A m-message at the desk?" A sudden flash of heat rushed through Lisle's body leaving her weak-kneed and stammering. Just like a kid! It *had* to be Hal. No, it didn't.

Andrea folded her arms and gave Lisle an agitated glare. "Yes, you know. The flashing red light on the phone means someone called and left a message. I buzzed the desk and it's for you, honey."

"Well, it could be Jon with another brilliant idea for the fall layout." Lisle quickly slipped into her bikini panties. "Or the PR coordinator with another assignment."

"Then why not just leave the message for either of us? No, I think it's Hal. But we'll never know by standing here speculating, will we?"

Lisle's hand clasped her forehead. "Oh, God, Andrea, what's wrong with me?"

"I would say, but we might not be friends much longer. Here, honey." Andrea thrust the phone receiver into her hand and punched O for her.

"This is Lisle Wheaton. Do you have a message for me?"

"Yes, Ms. Wheaton. Mr. Hal Kammerman requested that you call him in room 208."

"Thank you," she rasped, and dropped the receiver back in its cradle. Turning to her friend, she merely nodded. "I feel like a damned teenager, Andrea, all shaky inside."

"Hey, that's normal. A little emotion never hurt anybody. So call him," Andrea urged gently.

"Let me . . . calm down a minute." She began to pace about the room.

"The man is wise, Lisle. He knows better than to risk losing a good woman."

"Risk?" Lisle's nervousness turned to anger. "He doesn't have me to risk! Anyway, he's damned late. We're almost ready to leave. Damn it!"

Andrea waved a graceful hand in the air. "Oh, Lisle, don't give me those flashing eyes. Right now you're a pile of Jell-O at the thought of seeing Hal again. And if you have any sense in that pretty head of yours, you'll pick up the phone right now and call him! Well, honey, what are you waiting for?"

"You're right." Lisle pressed her lips together and placed her hand on the phone. A million thoughts raced through her mind. He had come, after all! Now what? This had been her dream for the last three weeks. Should she ignore him or see him? Rush into his arms? Shyly hold back? Should she even call? After all, he was late! Look what he had put her through. A few more hours, and they would have missed each other completely. Oh, but she *had* to see him. Just once more. They could talk, at least. Taking a deep, calming breath, she dialed 208.

When Hal answered, Lisle was suddenly speechless. And desperately nervous. After a pause she managed to blurt out "Hal? This is Lisle."

He hesitated only a moment. "Lisle! I hoped I would catch you."

"The photo sessions are finished. I'm packing to leave."

"Oh. Could we . . . talk before you go?"

"Uh, yes, of course." Was it disappointment she heard in his voice?

"Can I persuade you to stay, Lisle?"

She smiled, and the warmth of that smile could be detected in her response. "You could try." This was the Hal she remembered!

"I'd better warn you, m'lady, I can be very persuasive! And if persuasion doesn't work, I might be tempted to resort to the old Viking technique and fling you over my shoulder and carry you off to my lair!"

"I'd better warn you, sir, I can be a pushover! And I would love to be your captive!"

"Meet me in the bar in fifteen minutes."

She thought of her wet hair. "Make it twenty." Lisle pressed the button on the phone and looked at an eager Andrea. "I think it's reasonable to go ahead and cancel my flight to Dallas."

Andrea gave her a quick hug. "I knew it! I knew you'd come to your senses. That man cares for you, honey. And this time you'd better treat him right!"

"Oh, Andrea, this is so risky. I don't know if I'm doing the right thing."

"Yes, you are, Lisle. Just relax and let nature take its course."

"Andrea! That's advice I wouldn't give my own daughter!"

"But, honey, you're a mature, experienced woman." She winked as she crossed the room to the door. "You have a nice little vacation, now. I'll see you in Texas in a few days. The bellboy will be here for my bags in a few minutes. Will you make sure he just takes mine?"

Lisle nodded. "Have a good trip home. And, Andrea . . . thanks."

"Sure, honey."

The door closed, and Lisle flew about the room, hair dryer in one hand, deodorant in the other. Pausing before the mirror, she raked a brush through her hair, which fell in loose curls around her shoulders. She considered pinning it up into a knot on her head, then decided against it, not wanting to hide the gray streak in her luxuriant sable mane. Of course, photographers usually posed her with the gray streak showing. It was one of her chief assets, according to most. But for a brief moment she considered whether in fact it made her look older. When she saw Hal again, Lisle wanted to look as young as she felt inside! Young and happy and excited.

Nervously she dabbed on a little makeup and perfume, then straightened the pale blue turtleneck sweater that she wore over black slacks. She sighed into the long mirror. There, that would have to do. She wondered, with a giddy feeling, if Hal, too, had spent so much time preparing for this meeting. Instinctively she knew he hadn't. Men didn't get nervous about meeting women. At least, they didn't show it. As Lisle approached the bar she hoped *her* anxiety didn't show.

Across the room Hal waited impatiently for her arrival. He stared blankly out the window as the wind whipped up a swirl of brilliant leaves, blind to their magnificent colors or the impending storm. He could only think of *her*. Life had been an agonizingly slow succession of days leading up to this moment. A dozen times during the last three weeks he had picked up the phone to call Lisle. But something had held him back. He had wanted to send her flowers with a gracious note saying how much she meant to him, how revitalized he was with her. But he knew that would push her further than he dared to just yet.

She was reluctant, skittish even. He wasn't sure why—didn't know what inhibitions she had to shed before she could be completely free with him. But he knew he had to take it easy with her. No rushing. No pushing. Just gentle loving. Actually, he was damn lucky she had agreed to meet this weekend. Now there was hope.

Hal turned in time to catch Lisle's entrance into the bar. God! She was a beautiful woman! Her hair hung loose around her shoulders—so casual and sexy. The violet of her eyes was accented by a luscious blue sweater, and the elegant way she walked through the room caught everyone's eye. He wanted to bury his hands in her hair, to touch her . . . all over . . . to swing her around the room!

With all the control he could muster, Hal stood to greet her. "Lisle . . . you're lovely."

"Thank you," she murmured, breathless at the sight of

him in pin-striped slacks and an open-necked dress shirt. The vest was gone, as was the tie, and a small cluster of grayish chest hair was visible at the V of his open shirt collar. Her fingertips touched the back of his hand, and he bent down to kiss her cheek, very near the earlobe.

His lips brushed sensually over her skin, sending delicious tremors down her spine. She felt rather than heard his heated words. "I've missed you like hell!"

"I was afraid you wouldn't come."

"I thought I had missed you." He steered her to the cushioned seat next to him and took her hand, pressing his warm palm to hers. "I was contemplating a trip to Texas."

Lisle's eyes met his for a frantic moment. Oh, no! She didn't want him coming to Texas! That would dispel the magic. With feigned calm she said, "I'm glad you made it here, Hal."

"I had business in Philadelphia. In fact, I just finished with a meeting this afternoon, which is why I'm still in this suit. Then we ran into bad weather, and our flight was delayed. We just made it out before the airport was socked in. A storm is tracking up the coast. It should reach us sometime tonight." His blue eyes caressed her face. "I happen to have a bottle of Riesling if you'd like some company to wait out the storm."

"I'd love it." She smiled, remembering the storm on Grand Manan. "I hate to listen to those shutters flapping, all by myself." He brought her hand to lips that were velvety and tantalizing, making her long for more touching, more kissing.

"You'll never have to be alone, Lisle. All you have to do is call me."

"It sounds very reassuring. I'll remember your promise, Hal." In the past eight years there had been lonely nights, and days, when she longed for someone with whom she could share her experiences, talk over her private struggles

64

at work. Someone who could care about her joys and heartaches. Sometimes the loneliness was almost unbearable.

"Just remember me, Lisle." There was a certain poignancy to his request.

She met his blue eyes with frank honesty. "I'll never forget you, Hal. Our time in Grand Manan together was very special to me. And so are you."

The private moment was interrupted by a waitress who stood politely waiting to take their order. "What'll you have?"

"A little white wine, please," the model in Lisle ordered.

"I'll have V.O. and water."

"What, no blended grog?" Lisle smiled impishly at him after the waitress left.

"That's reserved for the Viking's lair. Here, in White Mountain country, you'll have to dream up a new fantasy. Maybe a mountain man or—"

"Bigfoot, perhaps? A big hairy beast?" She laughed aloud. Suddenly she realized that she hadn't laughed aloud or felt so lighthearted in weeks. Three, to be exact. "Hal, it's great to be with you again. I feel so—so young when we're together. I looked forward to seeing you."

"Does that mean I won't have to do much persuading to get you to stay?"

"I've already canceled my flight home," she said. "Is it too bold to admit I wanted you to come? And I want to spend the next few days with you?"

"Too bold? Hell, no! I'm very attracted to you, Lisle, and it's exciting to know you feel the same way. If you had refused to spend this week with me, it would be a tremendous blow to my ego." His eyes were intense as he admitted his own insecurity.

"Hal, surely you know I wanted to stay with you." She watched the lines of concern soften along his brow and realized they both had insecurities about their relationship. Perhaps he *was* somewhat nervous about this meeting, although for different reasons. When would they learn to communicate real feelings and real fears? Maybe this was a beginning.

"I don't know a thing until you tell me."

The waitress brought their drinks, and Hal shifted to sign the tab. Lisle watched his movements as he wrote, intrigued by the evident strength in his hands, and remembered how those hands had gently caressed her face and held her close.

As he sat near her, momentarily preoccupied with the bill, Lisle, who was lost in womanly imaginings, sought to recapture the memory of kissing him. She thought of the pleasure of touching his chest beneath his pristine white shirt.

And yet, looking at him now and thinking of him in such an intimate way, she realized that he was a stranger. Lisle wanted to know more about this man beside her, wanted to laugh with him and share stories. She longed for the feel of his body next to hers. Was that so bad—to want to share intimacy with a man she admired? To need it?

"Are you fantasizing again, Lisle? You have that faraway look in your eyes."

Lisle's eyes met his in guilty admission. Perhaps he knew what she was thinking! Until this moment, with Hal beside her, she had not allowed herself to indulge in such fantasies. And now it was written all over her face, she was sure. Before she could answer, her cheeks flushed hotly, not with embarrassment, but with the wrenching, all-encompassing longing of a woman for a man.

"I—I was thinking of you. Of us," she stammered weakly, unable to think of a quick way out.

He ran a finger across her pink cheek. "Not embarrassing thoughts, I hope."

"No. I'm too old to be embarrassed."

"Intriguing, then?" he guessed diplomatically.

"Hmmm, yes. Intriguing."

He raised his glass to hers. "Are you going to tell me your thoughts, m'lady? Or do I have to guess?"

She tipped her wineglass to his with a tiny clink. "Later."

They sipped their drinks in silence for a few moments, listening to the howling wind as it grew in intensity. A blanket of darkness spread over the mountains. Once again they were alone, just the two of them, away from the everyday world they knew.

Lisle could sense the aura of vigorousness emanating from Hal's body. She inhaled the heady aroma of his expensive cologne and longed to feel his strong arms around her. With a deep, trembling sigh she willed her racing emotions to calm down. The two of them would be enjoying each other soon enough.

"Lisle . . ." Hal took her hand and pressed it against his thigh. Hard and muscular, it radiated heat, which penetrated her palm.

She looked up, her deep violet eyes meeting his honest blue ones. Neither spoke for a full, tense moment.

When he did speak, Hal's voice was low and hoarse. "I want to make love to you, Lisle. Sitting here with you and sipping drinks and exchanging small talk is driving me crazy. I don't think I can be polite much longer. You know why I'm here."

Lisle swallowed heavily and dropped her eyes. "Yes, I know," she whispered. "I want you, too, Hal."

"Then what the hell are we waiting for?"

CHAPTER FOUR

Their lovemaking was a gentle contrast to the furious autumn storm that consumed the White Mountains that night. Hal was a skillful lover who knew when to hold back and when to move forward. Lisle found herself responding eagerly to his every tender touch.

Clothes quickly discarded, they were drawn inexorably together. Lisle sighed shakily and rested her hands on his chest as their flesh touched intimately for the first time. Her small breasts nestled against his chest, and she could feel the tickle of his crisp chest hair against her silky skin. Hal's body was compact and solid, athletic and strong—the durable form of a man of action. She liked the feeling and wanted him to know it, but she wasn't sure how to tell him. Communicating during intimate moments wasn't something she had ever learned to do. She pressed her entire length to his, hoping he would know how she felt by her actions, her eager compliance.

Hal's strong hands stroked the fine lines of her back, then moved downward to her waist and hips. Her skin was like smooth silk, meticulously cared for and inviting to the touch. He ran his hand down her back again, relishing her soft femininity. He wanted to touch her everywhere and ensconce himself in her satiny comfort, immediately gratifying his own needs. He trembled, for he knew he must wait. Waiting would yield far more satisfying rewards than a quick, grappling satisfaction.

Cupping the slender curves of her buttocks, Hal molded his male hardness to her feminine pliancy. His desire for her mounted with every stroke, every heated breath.

Lisle could feel the unmistakable fire of his aroused passion as their thighs met. She swayed erotically against him.

"Oh, God, Lisle, I want you so, it's hard to wait," Hal rasped as he kissed her ear and neck.

"Not too fast," she whispered. "I . . . I need a little time."

"I want to give you what you need, Lisle. Just tell me." He shifted away. He would give her time even though he was burning with thoughts of the imminent culmination of weeks of waiting and imagining. "What's your pleasure?"

Lisle had never made demands of a lover before and wasn't sure where to start. She hesitated, allowing her hands to slide up his muscular chest and across the breadth of his shoulders, enjoying the texture of his skin beneath her palms.

"Oh, God, Lisle—"

"Just touch me . . . like this." She took his hand and guided it.

Hal traced her slender curves with appreciative hands, seeking her warm and hidden places. "You are every bit as lovely as I imagined, Lisle. I want to touch you, to kiss you everywhere." He led her to the bed. "Will an insulated blanket substitute for the Viking's bearskin?" he asked teasingly, pulling her down with him.

She smiled. "I never cared much for bearskins, anyway. It's the Viking I want."

Hal's voice contained a closely held restraint. "Tell me when you're ready."

With fervent yet suppliant passion his lips met hers, and Lisle trustingly submitted herself to him, body and soul. Convinced that he cared about her feelings, she closed her eyes and enjoyed his maleness. Lisle's passions heated to a blazing fire as his gentle hands stroked her shoulders, her back, her hips. His tongue traced the edges of her lips, begging for entry. When she complied, taking his sweet force into her body, he plunged deeply, rhythmically. She swirled in the esctasy of his impelling kiss.

He covered her with warm caresses, and she moaned with answering pleasure. Lisle writhed tantalizingly beneath him, her breasts and belly and thighs working their sensual magic on his hard virile body.

Hal made low, growling sounds. "Oh, God . . . Lisle—"

His hands moved to her thighs, stroking the tender skin. Long-dormant embers rekindled to a roaring blaze that surged through her veins to the seat of her desire. Her breasts ached with longing, and she arched to meet his intoxicating manipulations as his velvet lips tugged her nipples to hard knots of desire.

His long fingers slipped past her waist to the soft, moist core of her sensitivity, and she gasped from the abruptness of his invasion. Lisle strained against his touch, then tried to pull away. But there was no escaping these erotic pleasures. His fingers worked magic, exploring her femininity, drawing from her the maximum of sensual pleasure. Soon there was no reluctance, no resistance. Lisle was both the Viking's captive and the victim of her own raging desire.

A sigh escaped her lips as she felt herself grow limp in acquiescence to his entreaties. The flames of a wildly burning fire flashed from the core of her being to the outer reaches of her mind.

"Hal, oh . . . don't stop . . ." she whispered, feeling the warmth that was now settling in her weak limbs.

Both his hands reached around to cup her buttocks, pressing her swollen softness to his hardness. "Ah, Lisle, just looking at you, thinking of you, has aroused me. But touching you has driven me crazy! I'm ready to explode! I can't wait any longer," he rasped thickly.

She touched his firm flesh, stroking and inviting with her

slender fingers. "Then come to me, Hal," she whispered needfully, enticingly.

He moved over her, forging them together in one fierce, plunging thrust. Lisle met his strength with a display of her own, sending them both into a frenzy of ecstasy and passion. Mindless for the moment, Lisle was only aware of the torch that enflamed them, bringing about a climax of indefinable exhilaration.

"Lisle, love . . ."

"Hal, Hal," she answered in a soft exclamation of joy. Lisle pressed her face against his heaving chest and relaxed, knowing splendid fulfillment.

Their fury was spent long before the storm's, and they lay wrapped in each other's arms, listening to the whine of the wind blowing around the quaint clapboard building tucked away in the mountains of New Hampshire.

Hal breathed with a masculine vitality that invaded Lisle's very being. She tried not to think of the marvelous spell they wove together, of the richness Hal added to her life. Mentally she denied having any deeper feelings than lust for this man who had just loved her so completely and now held her so securely.

But her body had responded too fervently for this to be a passion of the moment. The light in her eyes when she saw him, the racing of her pulse when she simply thought of him, and the unmistakable lilt in her heart when she was with him couldn't be denied. Her body betrayed those emotions she so desperately tried to hide.

The realization of how much Hal meant to her came about slowly—not in a sudden flash of recognition, but in bits and pieces. Their relationship had come about in bits and pieces too: Curiosity, fantasy, laughter, passion, caring, had come together to create a special core of happiness, one that she hoped would last. However, could this happiness they shared be continually tucked away and rediscovered whenever they chose?

71

Hal pulled her tight against his chest, fitting her back and hips snugly against his powerful chest. Warmed by the heat radiating from his body, she leaned against the cushion of male hair as they lay cuddled like two spoons.

"Lisle? Are you all right?" His voice rumbled through her.

"Hmmm . . ."

"I—I didn't intend for this to be so damned fast. Did you—"

"Yes," she answered with a smug smile, knowing his question before he could say it. "I'm fine, Hal. It has been a while, for both of us. I understand."

"No excuses. It was . . . barbarian. Too fast. Too rough. Next time will be better. I promise. I have never been like this with any other woman. You—you drive me beyond my limits."

"So your untamed passion is my fault, huh?"

"No. My fault. But you destroy my self-control."

"Should I be flattered?"

"You control me like no other woman ever has."

"But there have been other women. . . ."

"Yes," he admitted reluctantly. "I've shared a bed with a few women. But that's all it was. A few nights. A few brief flings. Nothing lasting. No one special. Not for many years."

"Do you think ours will be a lasting affair?"

"Oh, yes, m'lady. I can't get you out of my mind when we're apart. Having an affair was always something I shied away from too. Now, who could make me change my style but someone like you who called me your Viking and drew me into your wild fantasies."

"You are so dashing and handsome, I couldn't resist!" She stroked the arm and hand that encircled her waist. "What is your usual style, anyway, Hal? Swinging bachelor?"

Lisle could feel the deep reverberation of his chuckling response. "Was, my love. Past tense. Before you came along, I enjoyed my bachelorhood to the fullest. The freedom, the independence . . . the status. I have escorted many beautiful women to state dinners and company luncheons. But there was no obligation to take them out again."

"Aha! The local gigolo!"

"Hardly!" He laughed. "I'm selective about who I accompany to lunch, but damned particular who I take to bed. No one has ever captured me the way you have, my lovely, violet-eyed sorceress." His lips planted velvet kisses along her bare shoulder, on her neck, and in her hair. Lisle shivered, as Hal's hand cupped one of her breasts possessively.

"I'm the one captured here, remember? Not you!" She squirmed delightedly at the tickling touch of his lips on her skin.

"Hmmm, so you say. That's the way with you sorceresses. You make the poor man think you're the helpless one, captivate him, then you quickly enslave him!" His teeth slid across one bare shoulder.

"Ah, the spoils of victory make it all worthwhile!" She laughed. "The captive has become the captor! Seized, body and soul!"

"Oh, yes, my love. I couldn't stay away knowing you were here at this little mountain resort waiting for me! I wouldn't take the chance of losing you."

"Well, you did almost miss me! I was packing to leave when you arrived!"

"And what a miserable soul I would have been if I'd missed you. I can assure you there would have been a quick flight to Dallas for this poor captive! You've snared me all right." He hugged her tighter.

Immediately she stiffened. She didn't like his choice of words. "Snared" was a word men used to describe being married. And that was furthest from her mind. Plus, for Hal to consider coming to Dallas, to her *home,* would destroy their fantasy. It was important for her to keep their relationship separate from her family. "No, Hal! I don't want you to

visit me in Dallas. We'll just keep this . . . our little secret."

"Secrets are fine for now, Lisle. But I would as soon fly to
Dallas to see you as anywhere. What difference does it make
where we meet?"

"No!" she repeated. "I don't want it that way. I don't
want to involve anyone else in our little fantasy. Hal, you
promised—"

His voice was gentle, though he was clearly puzzled by
her stubborn resistance. "You're right, Lisle. I promised to
do it your way—either of us can say good-bye at any time.
But, Lisle, I hope you realize how special you are to me now.
I can't let you go so easily anymore. I'd like to think you feel
the same way."

"Oh, I do, Hal. It's just that my way is to keep our relationship very private." Lisle turned to face him. "You want
an honest admission? I'm damned glad you arrived when
you did. I was a nervous wreck all week thinking I would
never see you again, Hal. What we had on Grand Manan
was so wonderful, I want to repeat every second. But it
mustn't interfere with our other lives."

"What we had then can happen again, Lisle. We'll make it
happen."

There was a pause, as if he were deciding whether or not
to ask. "Lisle, have you had other affairs? I know I said I
didn't care before, but suddenly, knowing about the men in
your life is important to me."

Lisle started and made a tiny gasping sound. For a moment she just stared into his eyes, wondering what in hell
she would tell him. A quick lie? She was never very good at
that. Oh, God, she couldn't lie to Hal again. But the truth—
she couldn't tell him that either!

"Is that an unfair question, Lisle?"

"No, Hal, you deserve to know about my past." She fid-
geted, then decided to buy a little time. "I—I have to go to
the bathroom. Please excuse me for a moment."

When she returned, she sat on the edge of the bed and began pulling on her clothes determinedly. She would tell him—just enough to satisfy his curiosity.

"Lisle . . ." Hal put his hand on her bare back, and she took a deep breath, trying not to react to his touch.

"I, uh—actually I've had two affairs. The first was a couple of years after my husband's death. Before we became too involved and did anything rash like marry, I realized he just wasn't right for me. Our parting was a mutual decision. The other was . . . different. It was a terrible mistake."

Hal folded his hands behind his head and stretched back to listen. When she didn't continue, he encouraged her: "Why was it a terrible mistake?"

She shrugged and said bluntly, "It just was. We were ill suited to each other." *And that's putting it mildly!*

"Lisle"—his fingertips grazed her arm—"I thought you said I deserved to know about your past. You're being very vague."

"Well, I didn't ask you for the intimate details of your past relationships!" she snapped.

"I'm willing to give detailed reports." His tone was mildly humorous.

"No! I don't want to know about all your women! Could we go downstairs for dinner? I'm hungry."

"Nor do I want to know about all your men. But I would like to know why you're so touchy about the subject."

"I'm not touchy!" She paused and sighed. "All right, maybe I am. It was so recent. But he seemed to be the one I needed to boost my self-esteem. Trouble is, he didn't really care about me or my feelings. Turned out he was the worst thing possible for my ego."

Hal moved closer to her, his finger lightly tracing the outline of her cheek. "You're a very beautiful woman, Lisle. And a very loving one. I can't believe your ego needed boosting."

She had been through the reasons a thousand times in her

mind but came up with only a few substantial ones. Maybe Hal would understand. "In retrospect, I probably entered that relationship for all the wrong reasons. Loneliness topped the list."

"Sounds like a legitimate reason to me."

"But the others aren't. Being with him made me feel good. I'm sure I was using him. And I know he was using me."

Hal was quiet for a moment, then asked, "Your lover was younger than you, wasn't he, Lisle?"

She gave him a quick look, acknowledging his intuition. "Yes. How did you know?"

"I just guessed," he hedged gently. "It's quite common to want to be attractive to someone much younger. Many beautiful women are vulnerable to the flirtations of young men who think these women are younger than they really are."

Lisle pulled on her sweater and ran her fingers through her hair. "Remember the pilot on the flight to Grand Manan? I don't know what happened to me that day, Hal. I didn't really care about him, yet I just couldn't tell him I was old enough to be his mom!"

"I think I understand, Lisle. Men are vulnerable too."

"Even handsome, silver-haired men?"

"Especially silver-haired men! I'm no exception. But one day I met a certain lady with a streak of silver in her hair who turned me on quicker than anyone else could! Now, surely that flatters your ego!"

"Yes, you do more for me than anyone else ever has, Hal. You have brought a smile to my heart."

"Did this guy hurt you so badly that you didn't want to take a chance with me?"

She turned away from his penetrating gaze and slid her long legs into the dark slacks. "When you've been a fool once, you don't want to make a habit of it. I was very reluctant to try again. It's a big risk."

"I think you're still reluctant."

"Maybe," she admitted, not meeting his eyes.

76

Suddenly he was beside her, his hands gripping her forearms. He forced her to look up at him. "Lisle, are you sorry you took the risk with me?"

With an eagerness she couldn't hide, Lisle answered, "No, Hal. I have no regrets. It's been wonderful with you—" The rest of her words were smothered in the powerful kiss that engulfed them both.

Their lips met fiercely, drawn together by an overwhelming force. Her hands grasped at his shoulders, digging into the taut muscles with a desperate fervor that urged both his aggression and her compliance.

The kiss deepened, and Hal lifted her tight against him. Lisle shuddered as his tongue plundered the recesses of her mouth, promising even deeper invasions. Anticipation welled within her. She burrowed her fingers into the curling hair at his nape, pressing his kiss to her lips with all her strength. She moaned softly as an overwhelming desire to press him into her being surged through her. She felt as though she would scream if he didn't take her soon. She wanted to touch him everywhere and wanted him to return the pleasure.

As they plunged into passion's dizzying whirl, he lowered her slowly to the bed. "We'll have dinner late tonight," he murmured in her ear, first kissing the tender, sensitive areas along her neck, then returning to the honey of her moist lips.

"I prefer to start with dessert, anyway," she said teasingly, her white teeth tugging gently at his bottom lip.

"Every time we're together, I can hardly wait to make love to you!" He directed her hand to his heated, swollen groin.

She stroked him triumphantly, knowing that she could bring him under her sensual domination, just as he had certain physical powers over her. "No man has ever loved me as you do, Hal. There are no others—"

In quick order Hal dispensed with the clothes she had so recently donned, and kissed her all over until Lisle begged

77

for the fulfillment only Hal could give her. Their bodies blended into one beautiful song of love, reaching the ultimate in perfect harmony.

Dinner was very late that night.

The blustering storm lasted all the next day. In its wake a dusting of snow adorned the brilliant autumn leaves and green balsam firs. Their mountain rendezvous had been transformed into a fantasy world of unforgettable beauty. In the late afternoon Hal and Lisle took a walk in the sparkling Currier and Ives landscape near Sunapee Lake, then returned to their warm retreat, laughing and cold. Hot buttered rum would chase their chill, although Lisle did protest weakly that she should stick to white wine.

Hal settled the matter with a roaring "Damn the calories! Full speed ahead!"

She polished off two hot buttered rums, then laughed her way up the stairs and into his arms.

The next morning, huddled over a mug of steaming coffee that she was taking in bed, Lisle moaned, "Ohhh! What a fool I was! Two rum drinks? Hal, how could you let me do that? You know I'm not used to drinking."

He raised an eyebrow and peered at her, his skin still glistening with droplets of water from his shower. "I may be your lover, but I'm not your keeper. You're still in charge of taking care of that lovely body, my dear." He flicked the towel over his body, then moved across the room.

Her hand pressed the top of her head. "And a damn lousy job I did of it too. I can't believe you have already jogged this morning. Makes me tired to think about it."

He stepped into sexy navy-blue jockey shorts, then hovered over her, affectionately kissing her nose. "Is your headache bad?"

"Not so bad that I can't recognize how you look in those briefs! I just need another cup of coffee to get me going."

He poured more of the steaming coffee into her cup.

"Maybe a little outside activity would be good for you. Do you feel like tackling the mountain today? I'm sure the storm left enough snow on the slopes to make it possible to ski. The fresh air would be good for you."

"I'd love to, but I'd better stay away from skiing." Lisle paused and took another gulp of coffee. "If I broke an arm or leg, I couldn't work. Can't afford the risk."

He flicked on the electric shaver and leaned toward the mirror. "Hmmm. On second thought, in your condition you might run into a tree."

"What?" She grabbed a buttered blueberry muffin from the breakfast tray and threw it across the room at him.

"I said we must take care of your gorgeous body." He dodged the missile and pulled on her toes through the covers.

"Keeping in good shape happens to be the way I make my living!" she countered indignantly. "Normally, that is."

"As opposed to abnormally, I suppose? Actually, I was thinking of other reasons for keeping you in good shape."

"As opposed to normal conditions, smarty! And you don't fool me! Your motives for keeping me healthy are purely selfish! No headaches allowed!" She sank her teeth into the remaining muffin.

"Just to show you how wrong you are, my love, how about a drive over to the beach today? Maybe a sedate walk along the shore would be more to your liking. Certainly it isn't as risky as downhill skiing."

"New Hampshire has a beach?" She squinted her eyes at him to see if he was teasing.

He slid long muscular legs into his dark slacks. "Of course, the shoreline is only about eighteen miles long. It's the site of one of the original fishing settlements that branched out from Plymouth, Mass."

"Oh, Hal, I'd love that! Dallas is so landlocked, sometimes I just crave being on a beach and smelling that won-

79

derful salt air!" She sat up in bed, definitely perked up by the idea.

"Sometimes I crave you, but I'll yield to your whims this time, my dear."

"Don't you want to smell the ocean?" She looked at him as if he were daft.

"You forget where I live. Wilmington is a major seaport. I get about all the seaside aromas I want!"

"Oh, yes," she acknowledged weakly. "I'd forgotten."

He rolled his eyes. "Well, let's get on the road. I want you to smell the ocean before you go back to Dallas. You'll have to bundle up to your ears on this beach, though. It'll be quite cold for a southerner like you."

"I don't care. I'll like it," she promised, smiling happily. "Even if I have to bundle up to my ears."

They drove through the snowy pine forests until they reached the New Hampshire seashore. Dressed like two Eskimos, they walked along the beach. Lisle soaked up the salty winter air with enthusiasm. At Seabrook they marveled at the incongruous siting of a modern nuclear plant, which dominated the historic beach, alongside seaport shops that sold the memorabilia of ancient mariners. On the way back to the green-shuttered Sunapee Lodge, they stopped at a roadside shop to watch a demonstration designed to introduce tourists to the process of tapping. They saw actual maple sap flowing from the trees into buckets. Then they huddled beside a huge vat of boiling syrup, inhaling its marvelously sweet aroma.

"I'd like to bottle this flavor and take it home so I could spritz the air with it occasionally." Lisle laughed as they bought several quarts of the finest syrup ever to be dribbled on a pancake. "Then I could have this superb aroma, but not the calories!"

Hal steered her outside, into the fresh cold air. "Surely you can't resist eating some of this syrup of the gods! I'll be glad to help you work the calories off!" he said teasingly, and

80

tried to pinch a nonexistent inch of fat around her waist. "Aha, not bad! You take very good care of your body!"

"You'll be able to pinch more than an inch if I follow my natural instincts and eat this syrup along with the pile of pancakes it requires!"

"I'll keep you busy. Tomorrow we'll go hiking." He paused beside the car door and spoke with a sudden seriousness. "How long can you stay, Lisle?"

"Just for the weekend," she muttered, gazing up into his intense blue eyes.

"That isn't long enough." He opened the car door for her with a jerk. They both knew it wasn't long enough, but were determined to squeeze every bit of joy into the limited time they had together.

The weekend was gone before they knew it. Soon they would be boarding separate planes to journey back to their separate lives. So precious were their last few hours together that they experienced each passing moment with unflagging intensity.

"It's been a fantastic weekend, Hal. One I'll never forget." Lisle's hand explored the span of his chest, softly caressing the mesh of curly hairs.

A single masculine finger traced the line of her cheek. "Our time together just hasn't been long enough for me, Lisle."

"I know," she said sympathetically. "But I have to get back to the real world and work. Surely you do too."

He shrugged. "My consulting business requires lots of traveling. Back at the office in Delaware I just clear up paperwork and schedule my next assignments. Leaves me free to pursue my flights of fancy. And you." His hand slid around to the warmest part of her neck beneath her hair.

"What a lovely relationship we have." She spoke musingly. "Two separate lives brought together via flights of fancy."

"Which reminds me, when will we meet again? What is your fantasy for the next time?"

"Next time? I—I don't know. Do you want to meet again?"

"Damn right I do!" he thundered angrily. "Don't you?"

"Yes, of course," she said soothingly. She was beyond resisting him. Or of even wanting to.

"We have a good thing going, Lisle. I'm not ready to let you slip away yet."

"Don't talk so seriously, Hal. I want to keep our relationship on a fun basis. No commitments. If you want to back out, it's still okay. You know, this is just our little fantasy." She was trying to convince herself as well.

He gazed curiously at her. Why was she afraid of this relationship? It was almost as if she were reluctant to admit they even had one. She obviously approved of him, of what they shared, or she wouldn't be here. Lisle was a woman with a strong mind. She wouldn't stay with him if she didn't want to, nor would she agree to another rendezvous. Then what was troubling her?

He sighed and decided not to press her just now. "Whatever you say, Lisle. Where would you like to go?"

She stretched one long leg straight up and flexed it several times. "Well, we've been on the East Coast twice now."

"How about the West Coast next time?" he suggested.

"Sure," she answered. "Sounds fine. Where? When?"

"Let me think." He thought for a moment, then said, "I have business in L.A. the week of November twentieth."

She perked up. "Why don't we spend Thanksgiving together?"

"Great by me! Since it's a holiday, maybe we could squeeze in more time together. Can you get a few extra days off?"

"I'll try."

"What about your family? Will there be problems?"

She pursed her lips. "I'll think of something to tell them."

"Why not the truth?"

"Hmmm, maybe." The truth? Was her family ready for that?

"A whole month away." Hal groaned. "Can I last a month without you?"

"Of course, darling." She placed a cool hand on his forehead. "We have an exciting week to look forward to. L.A. is a marvelous place for a fantasy. Let's see, there's Hollywood, and all kinds of night life, and Malibu, and—and the ultimate fantasy!"

"What's that?" He looked curiously at the impish smile on her face.

"Disneyland, of course!"

"That Mickey Mouse and Donald Duck stuff? Lisle, surely you've outgrown them!"

"Outgrown them? I hope I never outgrow the fun and fantasy they represent! My favorite Disney character is Goofy. He keeps trying, even with all his inadequacies. He accepts himself as he is, and remains undaunted by what life hurls his way. But Disneyland isn't just funny characters, Hal. It's like entering another world!"

Hal took her hands and pulled her close. "Is that what you want, Lisle? To enter a different world with me?"

"I want"—she nuzzled his neck—"to put a little fun in your life."

"You have done that, my love. More than you'll ever know!" He reached out with arms of tempered steel to engulf her in a tight embrace, and his velvet lips met hers.

As he buried his face in her mass of fragrant hair, Hal couldn't avoid a puzzled frown. She was so passionate, so loving in his arms. And she came to him willingly. She seemed eager for their next encounter. Yet she refrained from making any commitment—even from taking their relationship seriously.

Why did Lisle continue to call what they shared a fantasy, a light affair? Nothing serious. Why wouldn't she attempt to make their affair something stronger, more meaningful? They both wanted, *needed,* a sharing relationship. Already they were committed to another rendezvous.

However, she still insisted on no communications when they were apart. No phone calls, no flowers, no sweet love notes. It was almost as if she were running away from love, via her own little flights of fancy. And he was running toward her love as fast as he could. Maybe it was risky for him too. But he was willing to gamble.

"Hal . . ."

His puzzled thoughts faded as Lisle writhed sensually against him. Her firm breasts taunted him, and her slender thighs invited him to scale untold heights of passion he knew only she could create. With every motion she asked—no, demanded—him to make love to her without actually saying it.

This would be their last time together for a month. His strong hands cupped her hips and lifted her firmly against him. She wrapped her legs around him, and their bodies merged with natural urgency even before Hal lowered her to the bed.

CHAPTER FIVE

During the ensuing weeks Lisle kept busy and tried not to think about Hal and their secret affair. It had become rather more than a brief fling, she admitted to herself, since they now planned to have a third assignation. Lisle actually looked forward to their next tryst in Los Angeles, that is, when she did allow herself to think about it.

However, Lisle's heart overruled her mind, and in quiet moments she reflected on the hours she had spent with Hal, the strength that pervaded her being when she was with him. He had a powerful, dynamic personality. Was that what had first attracted her to him? Or was it his distinguished good looks? When Lisle closed her eyes, she could see him clearly: the intense blue eyes, the straight nose, the chiseled chin. She could even recall the way her body felt when his strong hands caressed her and he lay next to her, aroused.

There were times, in weak, lonely moments, when Lisle wanted to call him. To touch him, if only with words. But they had made an agreement. No communications. Actually, it was she who had insisted, claiming it was very important to her to keep their relationship separate from her other life, her family. Perhaps she wanted to ensure against a reoccurrence of the pain Kaplan had caused them all, or simply to indulge herself in the fun and magic of flying off to meet her secret lover. It was exciting, she had to admit.

But niggling questions continued to plague her: *What place does Hal occupy in my life? Only my bed?* She tried to shake off these thoughts, for they could easily lead her to make a negative, even vulgar assessment of their relationship. In any case, she just couldn't find answers to them yet.

The Delaware sky was gray and drab above the city. For the second time that morning Hal Kammerman lifted the phone receiver and, again for the second time, crashed it down into its cradle. "Damn it, woman," he muttered to himself. "Why—why the hell—" Mentally he finished the thought: *Why the hell let this woman tell me what to do?*

His gaze dropped to the magazine lying on his desk. Lisle's violet eyes and sensuous mouth smiled up at him, as if daring him to risk it all by calling her. Here was his Lisle —the woman he had laughed with and loved—on the cover of a famous woman's magazine! Christ! What a surprise to find her smiling from a stack of magazines at the corner newsstand! She wore a deep purple blouse, a drapey silky thing that covered, but did not completely hide, her sexy body. And God, she looked great!

He had to talk to her, to tell her of his surprise. His absolute delight. Yet Hal stalled.

Hal Kammerman would pick up the phone and call almost any executive in the state without trepidation. He had consulted with heads of state and advised foreign dignitaries on management procedures; he knew several governors on a first-name basis. No one told Hal Kammerman what to do. In fact, they paid for his advice.

So why was he intimidated by Lisle Wheaton? If he wanted to talk to her, why not just put through a call to her? She was merely an attractive woman who had touched his life briefly. *Merely?* How could anyone be called a brief acquaintance when she dominated his every thought? Yet she remained on the fringes of his life, for that's where she chose to be. And Hal could do nothing to pull her closer. It was this helplessness that was so damned frustrating!

He stuffed his hands in the pockets of his expensive blue

pin-striped slacks and stalked to the window. Instead of the Wilmington cityscape, grayed and weathered, he saw her face. Those unusual violet eyes beckoned to him while at the same time they pleaded for his understanding and patience. They commanded him to keep his distance.

Damn right, she did intimidate him! If he called her, or wrote or sent flowers *to the one I adore,* she might back away. No, he could not bring himself to step beyond the boundary she had so firmly set.

It looked as though Lisle were afraid of their relationship. She hadn't said so, but he sensed it. She was still too skittish. While he feared losing her she worked to keep them from becoming too close. Why else would she act like a young colt, tentatively seeking his affection, then backing away and making ridiculous demands, asking that there be "nothing between us till we meet again." He could even hear her saying those words and then punctuating them with the trill of her taunting laughter.

Yet at times she could be a hellion! She was spicy and full of fun, a kitten needing to be cuddled. Lisle combined the best qualities of all the women he had ever known or loved in his lifetime: beautiful, smart, youthful, she had a zest for life that Hal had missed in recent years. Perhaps he had grown too set in his ways. That was why Lisle was so good for him. She jarred him loose from his old habits and brought fantasy into his life, as well as a delightful reality. When he was with Lisle, life was joyous again.

Hal turned away from his office window with a sigh. He wanted to tell her all those things now, not wait until they met in Los Angeles. A numbing thought struck! What if she didn't come? It was possible. He wanted her to know what she did to him, for him. Why *not* give her a call? He reached again . . . and paused, his hand icy cold on the receiver. Did he dare invade her reality? Her other life?

"God damn it!" Hal's loud exclamation was followed by the whack of his fist slamming into his open palm. He pushed his secretary's button on the intercom. "Take any messages, Faye. I'm going jogging!"

Between wintry storms Dallas could be sunny and warm in November. Lisle and Inga took advantage of this beautiful autumn Sunday by going for a walk in the little park behind Lisle's town house. It gave them a rare chance to talk privately, as Alex romped ahead chasing after squirrels, on his way to the playground equipment.

"How was New Hampshire, Mother? Were the trees at their peak? Was it cold? You haven't talked much about this trip."

Lisle smiled as carefully concealed thoughts of the weekend in New Hampshire with Hal surfaced in her mind. "It was wonderful. Yes, very cold. We had a huge storm that brought a smattering of snow, but not enough to stop daily activity the way it does here in Dallas. The leaves were spectacular, of course, especially with a light blanket of snow on them."

Inga gave her mother a quizzical look. "You sound positively dreamy. You used to complain when you had to travel in snow and storms."

Lisle asked brightly, "Did I complain about that? See how we change? Our opinions, our attitudes, even our desires. . . ." Oh, how her desires had changed in only a few short weeks!

"Well, you've really done an about-face. How was your show? Was it well attended up in New Hampshire?"

"The show? Oh, the Sunapee show. It was dynamite, Inga, fast-paced and elegant. I wish you could have been there. We really set them back on their ears in New Hampshire. They'll remember the Dallas-based models for a long time." Lisle smiled broadly.

"And what about the photo session? Are you pleased?"

"Oh, yes, but we nearly froze. We wore that bizarre collection of wild-animal-print lingerie and posed outdoors. The

88

crew spent one whole day raking and piling leaves. Then we put on our zebra hose and tiger bikinis and played in the leaves like kids! It was crazy. Somewhere in all that, the director assures us, there were some good shots.''

"My mother, the lingerie queen! I love it!" Inga said teasingly, then grew serious. "It's been hard, but you've helped break the age barriers in the modeling business. Now there's a chance for the attractive woman who's past forty. It's a tough path you've chosen, Mother.''

Lisle murmured sarcastically, "What's really tough is being the 'old lady' of the group.''

"You have never been an old lady, Mother! You are one of the youngest, most interesting people I know!''

"Thanks, Inga." Lisle smiled warmly. "That's quite a compliment coming from my own daughter. I'm determined not to let society or anyone dictate when I'll be 'old.' I have a certain obligation to myself to be the best I can be for as long as possible.''

"Well, you're one of the best in today's market. I must admit, it's a charge to see your mom's picture on major magazine covers, though. Not many twenty-four-year-olds can point to *Playboy* and say 'My mom was interviewed in this issue.' ''

Lisle folded her arms. "I am not ashamed of that interview. I'm still glad I did it, even though it caused considerable upheaval in the lives of some people.''

"Meaning Craig," Inga said scoffingly. "Well, Mother, you must admit, it's not the kind of publicity a rising young politician wants." She smothered a giggle. "Remember the morning Craig called to report the *Morning News* headline 'COUNCILMAN'S MOTHER IN *PLAYBOY*?'''

"But when people read the article, they went away thinking differently. I talked about age discrimination and what a struggle it is to break into fields like modeling where they judge everyone on youth. It just isn't fair! Agencies still concentrate on the young, slim model. Don't they realize that the majority of the buying public isn't twenty-one and skinny?"

"I thought Image International was softening on its age-discrimination policies."

Lisle shrugged. "Well, they're better than most. They can boast two models over forty. Andrea and myself. I'm still the oldest in the group. But, Inga, there are dozens of attractive women of all ages who deserve the opportunity to shine. When will the powers that be accept that and change with the times?"

"Like you, Mother?"

She grinned. "Yes. Like me. I've tried to change. It helps keep you from growing old."

"Well, you're far from old. In fact, you seem even younger now than ever before. You're just radiant, and have been since—actually, since your trip to Grand Manan. Now, after staid, old New Hampshire, you seem even happier, if that's possible."

Lisle looked at her daughter uneasily. She was hinting at something. "Work is going well, for a change. And you and Craig are doing okay. What more could I want?" Should she tell her daughter why she was really so happy? Could she tell Inga that there was another man in her life? Maybe Inga suspected it already.

"How can you say that? Except for Alex, my life is an empty shell!"

"Things will improve for you, Inga. Your divorce is so recent, it's still fresh and painful. All things change in time."

Inga sighed. "I suppose. Even your attitude about flying has changed. You've always hated it, but this time you couldn't wait to dash off to New Hampshire. And you stayed longer than I expected. I thought you'd be back by Thursday—Friday at the latest. When I received your message that you would be staying through the weekend, I was a little alarmed."

"Well, you shouldn't have worried, Inga. I just decided to

stay a few extra days." Lisle wondered if now was the time to mention Hal. It was getting hard to keep her secret hidden, for she did want to share the happiness he brought into her life. "Did you know that New Hampshire has a seacoast? It's only eighteen miles long, but some of the coastal cities date back to early Plymouth Rock days. Seabrook, with that huge nuclear plant near the beach, is a very controversial port.

"On the way back we stopped at one of those sugaring places and bought maple syrup. You would have loved it, Inga; the place smelled heavenly." Lisle's eyes twinkled with a special glow as she recalled that day with Hal and how they had fed each other maple candy.

"Why the editorial 'we,' Mother?" Inga spoke hesitantly. "Are you hiding something? You and who else?"

"What would I be hiding?" Lisle avoided Inga's questioning gaze. She knew her fantasy was up.

"Mother, I know this is none of my business, but my intuition has been working overtime. Are you—are you meeting another man?"

Lisle gulped. She should have known that Inga would eventually guess the truth. But so soon? How could she get around this? Should she follow her instincts and bare her heart to Inga? Or deny it? Lisle walked around a nearby bush, picking at its bare branches. She took a deep breath and answered in the only way she could: "Yes, Inga, I'm seeing a man."

Her well-kept secret was now revealed. Unfortunately honesty was one of her better traits: lies had a way of mushrooming beyond her control. She wished she could swear Inga to secrecy. But was that fair? Maybe it would be best to be open about the relationship. Surely her family would understand.

"Mother! I—I can't believe it! After all the agony with Kaplan! I'm surprised!" Inga's first words were scornful, and

Lisle felt like a scolded child, because deep down she knew Inga was right.

"I'm only human, Inga!" Lisle looked away. "I know what you're thinking. I swore I'd never have another affair. But . . . this man is different."

"So was Kaplan." Inga scoffed. "Well, who is this new one? Where is he from? How did you meet him?"

Lisle took a deep breath before answering. "I met him on Grand Manan Island."

"I knew it! And you planned another rendezvous in New Hampshire?" The question was an accusation.

Lisle nodded silently. Suddenly she was in the unpleasant position of having to defend her alliance with Hal. There was no gentle understanding coming from her loving daughter.

"Tell me more about him, Mother."

Lisle stiffened. She had already revealed more than she had intended, sooner than she had expected. "Listen, Inga, I don't have to list his credentials. He's—This man is my private business. I'd rather keep it that way, if you don't mind."

Inga modified her earlier sarcasm. "It's just that I'm concerned about you, Mother. I don't want to see you hurt again."

"I know, darling. And believe me, I want to avoid that too." She smiled wryly. "Here's a switch. I feel like a teenager, slipping off on a secret date and then trying to explain it to my mother."

Inga laughed lovingly. "And I feel like the mother whose only concern is the welfare of her daughter. Surely you understand."

"I hope you'll be patient with me, Inga. I don't feel easy revealing too much about him yet. The experience with Kaplan was too hard on me. On all of us. I appreciate your concern. Why, this little fling may fall apart next week. Who knows?"

"Is that when you plan to see him again? Next week?"

Lisle nodded quietly. "We're supposed to meet in L.A."

Inga reflected a moment. "Next week? You're going next week? Mother! That's Thanksgiving week! You'll be back in time for Thanksgiving, won't you?" She was suddenly dead serious.

"No, Inga. I'm afraid I won't be back."

"But who will do the family dinner? Who'll fix the turkey?"

"The turkey?" Lisle gave a small chuckle at the heartlessness of her own daughter.

"Well, I mean, you've always had the traditional Thanksgiving dinner, Mother," Inga explained, clearly ill at ease.

"I suppose you can start a new tradition," Lisle proposed weakly. "There isn't any special trick to fixing a turkey, darling. Why must we be hemmed in by old traditions, anyway?"

"But—" Inga was now sputtering. "We don't want new traditions! We've always had Thanksgiving dinner at your house! The children look forward to it."

"I'm sure that you and Craig and Veronica look forward to it. But I suspect the little ones don't even know the difference. They're only three and two."

"Oh, Mother!"

"Please, Inga, don't make a big thing of this." Lisle halted Inga's protest by placing a firm hand on her daughter's arm. "Why don't you get Alex from the playground? Craig and his family will be arriving soon for our Sunday supper. I'll go ahead and make the Waldorf salad."

Lisle turned away from her startled daughter and walked toward the town house. Her secret was out! No longer would her relationship with Hal be a clandestine affair, unless Inga kept quiet about the revelation. Could she trust Inga to keep this affair a secret known only to a mother and her daughter —two women who shared something private? Well, she would know soon enough, for Craig and his family would be there within the hour.

93

The Sunday-night suppers were another family tradition. They didn't occur every Sunday evening but did so frequently enough. Since Lisle was so busy, each of her children brought a dish or two, and they gathered at Lisle's house. It was a way of keeping the family close without creating too much work for any one of them. It was the Wheatons' version of dinner at Grandma's.

After they had eaten and the dishes had been stacked in the dishwasher, the adults congregated in the living room to chat over coffee while the two toddlers played with blocks and trucks on the floor. Inga had been unusually quiet, even tight-lipped, and Lisle feared the moment when her daughter would give vent to her anger. Oddly enough, it was the absurd subject of Thanksgiving turkey that brought her secret to the fore.

"How's your new job as councilman, Craig?" Lisle asked.

"Very good, now that the press has calmed down about your *Playboy* article." Craig leaned forward, elbows on his knees. He was a dark-haired, handsome man, and like his father, he was very ambitious. There were times, though, when his mother's unconventional activities created more attention than he needed. "Actually, Mom, it was a very good interview. I could have done without that picture of you in the nightgown, but what can I say? You looked pretty good."

"I'm glad you've calmed down, too, Craig." Lisle's comment brought laughter to the group.

"I've learned some important lessons about politics." Craig chuckled. "One is that you aren't responsible for your family. And the other is that you'll eat a lot of kielbasa to get elected! In fact, right now our freezer's full of enough links to feed an army! How would you like Polish sausage for Thanksgiving?"

"Sausage? No, thanks!" Inga exclaimed. "We want the turk—" Her voice broke, and Lisle knew she had just remembered that her mother wouldn't be with them for the holiday.

"You'll be pleased to know that I already have the turkey for our Thanksgiving dinner," Craig announced proudly. "It was a gift from the Turkey Growers' Association. It's frozen, and I'll bring it over later in the week so you can thaw it here at your house."

"Don't bother." Every head turned toward Inga, who had uttered the sharp words.

"What the hell is that supposed to mean?" Craig snapped at his sister. "I thought you wanted—"

"Don't bother bringing the turkey here, because Mother isn't going to be home during the holidays!" Inga explained sourly.

Lisle sighed. She had known all along the secret would be revealed. And Craig and Veronica deserved an explanation, especially now that the beans had been spilled.

"Do you have to be out of town again, Lisle?" Veronica asked politely.

"Yes, Veronica, but it's not because of business."

"What do you mean, Mother?" Craig asked. "Why are you going, then?"

Lisle hesitated, toying with her blouse. *How do you tell your son and his wife that you're having an affair?* She hadn't done such a great job explaining it to her daughter.

Into the interval of silence in which Lisle gathered her wits and her words, Inga inserted, "Because she's meeting a man."

For a full minute the answering silence was overwhelming as Inga's flat statement settled over the small group.

Suddenly Craig exploded. "Good God, Mother! Do you mean you're having another affair? How could you? Do you know what the press would do with this titillating bit of information if they ever got wind of it?"

"Craig, don't be such a prude. I thought you said you'd learned that you aren't responsible for your family."

"Well, hell, most politicians don't have to worry about their mother's activities!"

"Most politicians don't have Lisle for a mother!" Veronica added, looking at her mother-in-law admiringly.

"Actually, Craig, I'm very discreet. The press won't get wind of this one, I swear! No one, outside this room, need ever know."

"Oh, don't bank on it! You do happen to be something of a celebrity in this town. Those gossip columnists find out everything! Anyway, I can't believe you didn't learn anything from past experience. Look what happened to you with that Kaplan fellow. I don't want you hurt like that again."

"I'm perfectly capable of handling my own affairs, Craig." Lisle stopped short of smiling impishly at her unfortunate choice of words.

"This isn't funny, Mom," he snapped, suddenly taking on the appearance and opinions of a much older man. "Have you forgotten so soon how Kaplan manipulated you? God! I hated him for that!"

"Please," Veronica pleaded, "let's not argue about Lisle's personal life. This is her business. She's independent. Let her lead her own life."

"I can't believe your simplistic viewpoint, Veronica." Craig cast his wife a searing glance. "This is *my* mother we're talking about. Just who is this new man, Mom? What does he do? Where the hell is he from?"

Lisle took a deep breath and began to tell them a few facts about Hal Kammerman, the new man in her life. They deserved that much, at least. She knew that her children cared what happened to her, and just wanted to protect her, even though their reactions did seem a bit harsh. She ached inside, seeing what turmoil her little fling was causing the family. Should she back down now? Should she call Hal and cancel their plans?

"You go right ahead, Lisle, and have a nice Thanksgiving

with your . . . uh, friend," Veronica said soothingly. "We'll miss you, but we'll manage just fine. We can have Thanksgiving dinner at our house."

"But who will fix the turkey?" Craig protested. "And the pies? Mother always does those. It's tradition."

Lisle rolled her eyes. Was it the fixing of the turkey, the abolished traditions, the press, or real concern over their mother that prompted her children's protests over her affair? What about her inner feelings? No one stopped to consider her. They only cared about food and . . . whether they would be embarrassed by her newest activity!

Lisle stood up, squelching the strong desire to march upstairs and leave them all. What she really wanted to do was to call Hal—to reach out to him for the support she knew he would give her.

"I'll fix the turkey," Veronica announced firmly. "You can help with the dressing, Craig. And Inga can be in charge of the pies."

"Pies?" Inga wailed, turning a near-panic-stricken face to Lisle. "Mother . . ."

"It's not that hard, dear." Lisle tried to reassure her quickly. "Use iced water for the crust and don't overwork it. Don't add too much spice to the pumpkin. Cinnamon, with just a little nutmeg. Easy on the cloves."

Inga nodded seriously, taking mental notes of her mother's quick directions.

Veronica added reassuringly, "You'll do just fine, I'm sure, Inga. Now, don't you think we should go home? We've caused enough rumbling for one evening. Lisle can probably use some peace and quiet. Anyway, it's time to get the little ones ready for bed. Lisle, I hope you have a good Thanksgiving. And don't worry about us." She hugged Lisle, then beckoned to Craig.

Lisle looked dubiously at her pretty daughter-in-law. Could it be that Veronica was the only one there who understood?—who actually cared about her feelings? Was her children's vision clouded by selfishness? Was it Veronica alone who could express the sincerity that she actually wanted to hear from all of them? "I appreciate your support more than I can say."

"We'll take care of the food, Lisle. You have fun in L.A.," Veronica said, then added in a whisper, "I wish *we* were going away somewhere."

"Thank you," Lisle mumbled, trying to muster her dashed spirits. Although the other two hugged her, they did so in a perfunctory way—with no discernible warmth or feeling.

She watched as they left the house still conversing about the holiday meal and who would fix what dish. Somehow, Lisle had not thought that the food would be such a problem. It had never been so in years past. But then, she had always been around to keep the traditions. She turned away from the door and quickly wiped her tears. Damn! Maybe . . . maybe she should call Hal and cancel. . . .

But, no! What had happened to her determination? She had always sacrificed for her family. Now it was time for her to lead her own life. To hell with pies and Thanksgiving turkeys! She would go to Los Angeles with Hal and never look back!

CHAPTER SIX

Hal met her at the Los Angeles Airport.

Lisle hurled herself into his arms and buried her face in his chest, brazenly ignoring the airport crowds around them. He was her escape, a refuge, a solid fortress from the discriminatory, judgmental world. She held him tightly, almost frantically, as if she would never let go. Just touching him was exhilarating. She wanted him to whisk her away in his arms—away from the real world, away from the demands of her work and her children.

Lisle slid her hands under Hal's suede jacket, feeling the strength of his ribs beneath his shirt. She breathed in deeply his clean, masculine scent. Oh, yes, Hal was warm and strong and good for her. Lisle was suddenly very glad that she had defied her children and flown to meet him.

Hal abandoned his usual public reserve and wrapped his strong arms around Lisle. He nuzzled the fragrant dark hair that fell over her ear, and murmured in it, "Lisle, love, I've missed you so much."

"Hal . . ." Her words were muffled, spoken as they were against his chest. She could not pull herself away from him, could not force herself away yet. He was her dauntless Viking, and she didn't dare let go, or else she might crumble all alone. When Lisle finally raised her face to his, it glowed with a love she couldn't hide. "Hal, it's been so hard, missing you and not knowing what to do! Do you realize this is Thanksgiving week?"

"Yes," he said gently, puzzled by her intensity. "That's the way we planned it, remember?"

Lisle nodded and swallowed hard. She hadn't planned on the hassle with her family, or the guilt she wore so heavily.

He caressed her chin with his thumb and forefinger. "Lisle. God, you're beautiful! How have I stood it away from you . . . away from this . . ." And his lips blended with hers in a brief, magical kiss.

Sudden tears rose in her large violet eyes, for she knew that being with Hal was worth it all. One moment with him, and the guilt was washed away, the arguments were forgotten. She needed his attentions, his devotion—yes, even his love.

Hal's thumb rubbed away an errant tear. "Hey, m'lady, crying already? That's supposed to happen at the end, not the beginning. This is just the beginning for us. Look at that beautiful California sunshine! It's going to be a great week, Lisle. Just the two of us, doing what we want to do."

She smiled happily, and the tears glistened in her violet eyes. "It'll be a beautiful week even if it rains every day! What's important is that we'll be together! I'm really glad I came."

Hal arched a bushy gray eyebrow. "Was there any question about your coming? I can tell you right now, love, I would have been one damn mad Viking if you hadn't walked down that concourse today! Have you ever seen a Viking when he's mad?" He halted, then with a devilish twinkle in his blue eyes he muttered between clenched teeth "Vicious!"

Lisle laughed, a lighthearted joy welling up inside her. "Well, I'm glad I saved us both that awful experience!"

"Me too!" He hugged her again, then arm in arm they headed through the airport for the luggage-claim area.

They piled her bags into Hal's rented car and hit the hectic L.A. freeway. "I hope you'll always remember this trip to Los Angeles, Lisle. We are going to have a ball! Anything your heart desires is available here, my love!"

"Just being with you again is for me the ultimate fantasy, Hal."

"My God! Where's your imagination, woman! In this town you can do anything you want! Any of your wildest fantasies can come true in California! It's got everything from Disneyland to Hollywood!"

She laughed and moved closer. "I must admit I love Disneyland. I guess it's the kid in me."

"Then we'll go, if it's something you really want to do, Lisle."

"It is. But only because I want to enjoy it with you, Hal. I want to see your face when you're going down the Matterhorn."

"Do you know what fun you've added to my life, Lisle? I must have been a dull stick-in-the-mud when you met me."

"I won't comment on that!" Lisle laughed and placed her hand on his arm. "Hal, I really want to be with you on this trip. We don't have to go anywhere, you know. We could just stay in the room and have our meals sent up, and I would be sublimely happy. Actually, I'll be a little disappointed if we don't have a storm. That seems to be our pattern."

"I doubt if southern California can come up with anything to compare with what we had in New Hampshire or Grand Manan, unless, of course, earthquakes are your style! So, I guess we'll have to make our own storm!"

"Corn-y!" She laughed, then leaned over to kiss his cheek. "That's why I came out here, you know! To create an earthquake with you!"

"What a sexy offer! Is this the same sophisticated lady who appears on the covers of national magazines? *My Lisle?*"

"Perhaps I should have warned you about that latest photo."

"The one with the purple scarf? I was somewhat surprised when I walked up to the newsstand," he acknowledged. "It's strange to see someone you think you know intimately on

101

the cover of a magazine. Suddenly she's so . . . public. I must be competing against some pretty heavy odds just to have you here with me, Lisle. More than once I've asked myself 'Why does she insist on meeting like this? And why me?' "

"Fun and fantasy!" She laughed lightly. Hal didn't answer her, and Lisle wasn't sure if his tight-lipped concentration was due to the traffic as he battled his way across town, or to her breezy comment. "Look, Hal, don't delve too deeply for answers, because I don't have them right now. I only know that you give me so much, just being yourself. I love being with you, and that's why I'm here. It's as simple as that."

"I have the feeling you lead two separate lives, Lisle. And I'm only in one of them."

"You may be right, Hal. There are times when I feel as though I'm being pulled in many different directions. But surely you know you aren't competing with anyone, Hal." *Only my family!*

"I'm prepared for the battle, Lisle. I don't intend to let you slip through my fingers."

"You don't see me trying to slip away, do you?" She squeezed his hand.

"No, not completely away. But I do see you keeping me at arm's length. You can't imagine how many times I've wanted to call you during this last month!"

"Hal, I explained that—"

"I know," he said quickly. "But I don't like the rules of our game anymore. I want to be in control."

She looked down at her hands. He was right. Until now, she had been calling the shots and he had been playing it her way. But was it really fair to him? Hal was nothing like Kaplan. And whatever made her think this affair would have the same unhappy consequences as the disaster with Kaplan? It definitely would not!

"Lisle, I'm sorry. I shouldn't have jumped on that issue so

102

soon. I've known your feelings about this all along. Now I suppose you know mine."

She reached to caress his hand, then interwove her fingers with his. "You're right, Hal. This is something we definitely should discuss. Maybe later."

"Yes, later." He nodded shortly and wheeled into the entrance of an elegant hotel in the Spanish style. Palm trees and flowering azaleas graced the entrance.

Lisle entered a room more gorgeous than any she could ever have imagined. Hal went over to the window and opened the drapes to reveal the astonishing view of the Hollywood Hills, which lay before them. Lisle exclaimed in delight, "Oh, Hal, this is gorgeous! Just look at that view of the city!" She slipped out of her shoes and wiggled her toes in the plush carpeting beneath their feet. "Feel this thick carpet! Luscious!" She threw herself into his arms with an enthusiasm she could not contain.

The pressures of her job, and the sharp words she had traded with her son and daughter, were forgotten. There was no thought about the future—their future. Only the present mattered as Hal held her close. "Lisle . . ."

She stretched her arms around his shoulders. "This is lovely. It's going to be a great week for us. I feel like a princess."

His lips were very close to hers, and she could feel their softness before they actually touched. "You are beautiful, my love. And so is what we have together."

"Love me, Hal . . ."

Her eyes were pleading, yet they held a flicker of reticence. Why couldn't she let go completely? Why couldn't she give herself to him, to their love?

But he didn't question her. He couldn't deny her request. His hands were hot on her back as he pulled her to him, melding their pliant shapes. "Lisle. Oh, Lisle. It's been agony without you."

His lips covered hers in a vigorous shoving of tender flesh

against her teeth. With sudden passion rising in her like a jet of water issuing from a fountain, she opened her lips to accept his velvety probing. As his tongue plunged into the sweet recesses of her mouth, Lisle swirled with dizzying desire. She wondered how she had endured this long without his love. Within moments she slipped into the now-and-forever fantasy of being in Hal's arms. They both felt the power of the fantasy, along with the growing urgency to make love.

They hurried to undress, dropping their clothes in an uncharacteristic heap at their feet. Tormented by a passion held in check for a month, they engaged in the act of making love, each one blending with the other. His kisses spilled over her, making her hunger for the delicious feast that his body would offer. Her fingers passed lightly over his turgid, masculine form, eliciting low groans of pleasure from deep within his chest. Heady with the intoxicating power of love, Lisle pushed him back against the elegant tapestried bedspread.

"This one is mine," she whispered hoarsely in his ear as she braced her hands on his shoulders and slid her lithe body over his taut maleness. His hands rested on her hips, guiding, applying pressure, seeking her warmth. She lay almost flat on him, her belly enticing his, the motion of her hips creating sweet, tormenting friction between them.

"Oh, God—Lisle!" His voice was a groan.

"You're mine to love," she murmured, her hands wreaking havoc with his tightly held restraint. Digging into his muscles with fingers that left barely visible indentations on his skin, she raised her hips and slid over him. Moaning in ecstasy, he began to rock slowly beneath her.

Their passion mounted like an approaching storm, and the motions of their lovemaking were frantic and feverish. Unhurriedly the storm subsided, leaving them drenched but fully sated in its wake. Now they floated in a gyre of semiconsciousness, rotating ever so slowly until at last they came to rest.

The afternoon California sun streamed through the open-curtained window to bathe two bare bodies in its warmth. There was no movement, for to move would be to destroy their magic circle.

They lay entwined, her legs wrapped around his, her arms encircling his chest. "Oh, Hal," she said, her voice muffled as she bent toward his shoulder. "It's better than I imagined. Better than I remembered."

He turned to his side and cuddled her, kissing the perspiration-dampened curls at her temple. "Lisle, my dear, don't deny what we have. It's too much like love—"

She pressed two of her fingers to his lips and said, "Don't, Hal—" Oh, God! She didn't want to hear that from Hal! Not yet! Their affair was too much fun to be serious. Too wonderful to become enmeshed with the real problems of life, like work and children. And love. "Don't ruin our fantasy!" She squeezed her eyes shut and laid her head against his chest, kissing a muscled spot on that cushion of matted hair.

Lisle took a warm bath after Hal left to finish up some business in town. Relaxing in the deep tub, she wondered about their future. They would have to come to terms with their relationship sometime. How serious was it? Was he pressing her for answers? She didn't have any now. But what if they became serious about their relationship? What in hell would they do about it? He lived and worked in one place. She, in another. Love would really complicate things!

Actually, there was no place in her life for a man now. Lisle had already decided that. Was it unrealistic to want things to stay as they were between Hal and her—to want to carry on an affair that allowed them to pursue their flights of fancy? Or would they have to end it all? She took a quick breath. Could she really face life without Hal, now that she knew him and had loved him? Knowing what she had missed all those years without him made their present relationship all the more valuable.

Lisle closed her eyes and sank deeper in the tub. She didn't want to think about change.

That evening they had drinks at the Cock 'n' Bull, a pub on Sunset Boulevard where the atmosphere was cozy but vety, vety British. Then they strolled down the street to dine on Scandia's famed Swedish meatballs. Afterwards they drove around the hills above the city to see the scenic view at night. Actually, though, it was the ecstasy of lying in each other's arms all night long that they both craved, and one meeting of their eyes communicated their desire.

"Lisle . . ."

"Yes," she answered knowingly. "Let's go back."

At the window, between the drapery and the wall, a faint streak of morning light wedged its way into the room. Hal drew his finger around her ear, then across her hairline and her neck. "What are you really like, Lisle?"

She moved against his bare chest. "What's wrong with you? This is the real me. There is no quicker way to get to know someone than to live with him. Or her."

"Well, I haven't lived with you enough to know all about you. I mean at home. What are you like around the house? I know you intimately and have been with you for several days at a time, yet I feel as though I don't really know you. What are you like, day in and day out, when life gets to be a dull routine?"

She reflected for a moment. "Like anyone else who works, I'm not at home a lot. And I must admit, because of my job, life is never very routine. Or dull. I travel quite a bit and work odd hours. Since my children are grown, I don't need a large place anymore. So I have a town house that's perfect for me." She caught herself before she said, It's just big enough for one person. "What about you, Hal? What kind of house do you have?"

"Me?" He chuckled ruefully. "I rattle around in a large two-story colonial-style house. It's far too big for me, so I have a live-in couple who help keep it up. Actually, the only time it seems right is when I have overnight guests or a party. It's made for large gatherings of people, not a bachelor who occupies a small, limited space."

"Then why do you have such a big place?" Lisle asked him.

He shrugged. "I don't know. It's the home Beth and I lived in, and I just never moved. Should have, I guess."

Lisle stroked his chest. "I think I can understand, Hal. It's probably comfortable where you are."

He sighed. "Yes. That's it. It's a lovely, comfortable home."

"And," Lisle added, "change is risky. What if you had changed to a place you hated? You already knew you liked this one. Plus, moving is traumatic and a hell of a lot of trouble. I can understand that."

"Yes, I guess it comes down to a fear of the risks involved. I never considered it that way, Lisle."

She caressed his stubbly chin. "We all have that fear, Hal. Fear of taking risks." Lisle pressed her mouth against his chest, momentarily lost in thought. That was her problem, too, only it had nothing to do with a house. She was fearful of emotional risks and wanted to avoid the inevitability of reality. That was why she preferred to meet Hal in a faraway place. To her way of thinking, that reduced her gamble. He could be her fantasy lover, always waiting to sweep her away to romance. They could forget the real world during the time they were together. He could be the daring Viking of her imagination; she, the willing captive.

"You still haven't told me about yourself, Lisle," he grumbled. "Not really. Let me guess what you're like around the house. You're a compulsive cleaner. And you spend your evenings studying the latest fashions and listening to classical music."

"The illusions of our men." She chuckled warmly. "How very wrong you are! I do like things around me to be neat,

107

and usually keep my home pretty straight. But I save the real cleaning for my housekeeper, who comes twice a week, mainly because I don't have time for it. And as for how I spend my evenings, I attend a small jazzercise group in aerobics twice a week, when I'm in town. We dance to rock music. Michael Jackson is a favorite, but we go for anybody with a good, strong beat. Sorry to disappoint you, but there are no knitters in my crowd!"

"Next you'll be telling me you and the gang are learning to break-dance!" He laughed.

She shrugged. "Not yet. But who knows?"

"No quiet evenings by the fireside, reading?"

"I don't even have a fireplace. And there aren't many evenings when I have time to sit around and read. But when I do . . ." She paused and chuckled. "It's a historical romance. I love a delicious escape to another time and place."

"The ones where the pirate kidnaps the virgin?"

"Yep! Or the Viking rescues the beautiful maiden from her evil stepfather! Or the wealthy landowner's son takes over the lovely heroine's ranch, and later they strike oil on the South forty. I love a good fictional escape. You should know that by now."

Hal said with a droll smile, "Yes, I should have guessed."

"Then there are my plants," she acknowledged. "They bring me back to earth, serenely. I get a great deal of satisfaction from them. They are quiet, trusting souls, just waiting there for me, and I take very good care of them when I'm in town. When I'm away, my neighbor gives them rudimentary care, just enough to keep them exuding oxygen. Then, when I return, they are so grateful!"

"My God, you do have a wild imagination, woman! You talk about these plants almost as if they're human. Do you also play them your favorite rock music?" he inquired teasingly.

"Oh, no! I don't want to shock them out of their pots! I

play them something soothing and romantic like Placido Domingo. His voice seems to make them thrive."

"You've finally touched on something on which we can both agree. Placido Domingo I find enjoyable. I can't say if you and I are compatible on a daily basis, though. There are so many differences. My house is large and roomy; yours is obviously small. I prefer my plants outside, in a garden tended by someone else. Your plants are in the house. Of course, you know jogging is my main physical activity, and I despise rock music. As for reading, *Time* and the *Wall Street Journal* are tops. One out of six isn't bad, is it?"

She narrowed her eyes. "You're digging for something, Hal Kammerman. What difference does it make? What are you after?"

"Just curious."

"There are some serious snags in this compatible little web you have woven. I have no desire to live in a huge, two-story house."

"You'd get used to it. I have a live-in maid and gardener."

Lisle sat bolt upright. "Oh, no, I wouldn't! Don't talk that way. I have no desire to move. I—I like it the way it is now —our meeting in wonderful places. Look at the risks involved in living together."

"Still living out your fantasies, Lisle?"

"Don't get serious about me, Hal. I—I can't handle it yet. My family can hardly abide our present situation, and I don't think I could bear anything else now."

"Good. So you've told them about us."

"Yes. They—they found out."

Hal could feel the negative vibes coming from her and knew it hadn't gone well. That explained why Lisle had been so uptight when she arrived. When would she ever feel secure enough in their relationship to tell him the personal things that troubled her? "And what did they say?"

"They asked who was going to fix the turkey."

"The turkey? What turkey?"

"The *Thanksgiving* turkey! Remember what week this is, Hal. Most families get together to eat, including mine."

"Damn! Is that all they said?"

"No. They also wanted to know who would fix the pies." Her large violet eyes grew sad.

"What did you tell them?" He knew that these grown-up children had a great deal of influence over Lisle and could affect his relationship with her.

"I told Inga how to make a pie shell without overworking it."

"My God, Lisle! Can't you be serious?" Hal's frustration was mounting. "I mean about us! What about us?"

She looked deeply into his eyes. "I told Veronica and Craig how to cook the turkey upside down so it would be nice and juicy . . . because no matter what they said, I was meeting you for Thanksgiving."

"Lisle," he murmured as his arms embraced her, pulling her back down on the bed with him. "For God's sake, please don't let them come between us."

"There hasn't been time," she said honestly, "for the full repercussions of the situation to reveal themselves. My family just found out about us a week ago. My daughter sees it as an invasion of her relationship with me. My son has recently been elected to a seat on the county council, and I can tell you now that he is none too happy with his mother's activities. Remember the *Playboy* article?"

"He was mad, huh?"

"In the immortal words of the angry Viking, vicious!"

"But that article was about age discrimination. Damn good too."

"Oh, Craig changed his tune when he read it. But there were still the photos."

"Damn good photos too," he said, nuzzling her neck. "So you defied your family to come out here?"

"I'm determined to live my own life, regardless of what

my children think. I wanted to be here with you, so I am. You're worth it all, believe me."

"Worth the risks involved?" he asked quietly.

"Oh, yes! That is, if you'll agree to take me to my favorite fantasy place today."

"We'll do whatever your imagination craves, m'lady."

"I want to go to Disneyland!"

"Whatever you want . . ." His kisses rained over her face and down her neck.

"Oh, Hal, come on now. We have to shower and get ready. What time is it? Seems awfully dark out there."

"It's just the lining of the drapery—it dims the natural light." Hal rose reluctantly to peer out the window. "No, it isn't. Looks like rain," he announced.

"Switch on the TV. We'll see what the weatherman says," Lisle advised, snuggling under the covers until Hal came back to join her. With great seriousness they studied the weather maps showing the front that had blown in from the Pacific and now shrouded Anaheim with the threat of rain. They debated for half an hour before deciding to go to Disneyland anyway. Rain, be damned! Together they would take the risk.

Apparently, over half of the potential Thanksgiving Day crowd felt the risk was too great, for Hal and Lisle had the whole Disneyland Park practically to themselves. There was no waiting in lines that wove through the French Quarter or around the Matterhorn. They munched California's version of New Orleans doughnuts and drank hot, black coffee, similar, but not equal to, the rich chicory type found in the real French Quarter.

Wrapped in each other's arms in the blackness of the Haunted House, they grabbed kisses like two lovesick teenagers. Then, in the make-believe world of pirates, they stood on the bow of the outrigger *Columbia* as it explored the wilderness. Lisle even managed to drag Hal aboard the Thunder Mountain Railroad for "the wildest ride in the

West!" Cruising the undersea grotto of the Pirates of the Caribbean, they were whirled back in time, to experience adventure on the high seas.

"You know, this is a secret fantasy of some women," Lisle whispered. "To be captured by a pirate and taken to a beautiful deserted island in the Caribbean!"

"Is it yours?" he murmured.

"No. Mine is the Viking fantasy." She laughed lightly. "Handsome. With graying hair along the temples. And strong, but gentle. Like you, Hal." She ran her fingers through his hair.

"You have a strange imagination, woman." Even in the darkness of the pirates' grotto he was true to his conservative nature.

"Only because it gets me through the rough times."

"Your imagination?"

"My fantasies."

"Well, then I want to be a part of your fantasies," he said firmly.

"Oh, you are, Hal. You most definitely are."

"But when are you going to take me seriously, Lisle? When are you going to put me in your real world, where I belong? Where I want to be?"

Lisle looked away into the darkness, knowing there was no place for a dashing pirate in her real world. Their boat rounded a corner, and they found themselves in the midst of a land-to-sea battle with cannons firing all around while a replica of New Orleans blazed beside a make-believe pirate ship.

Another few turns of their phantom vessel, and they saw daylight. Their ride through the turbulent, fantastic Caribbean was over. And Lisle couldn't help wondering if the same would soon be true for their affair.

CHAPTER SEVEN

They stood close, hands clasped, oblivious to the noise and people surrounding them at the airport. The holiday crowd pushed by, shoving and knocking, but they pretended not to notice. This was IT, and they wanted to enjoy their last moments together to the fullest—for the memory of these precious moments would be all that they would have in the weeks to come.

"I'll see you in three weeks. We'll spend Christmas together in Aspen. What could be more wonderful, Hal?" Lisle smiled wistfully, her eyes alight with encouragement. She knew his feelings and frustrations. He wanted more time together and let her know it in no uncertain terms. If nothing else, this trip had increased communications between them. At least, on Hal's part, it had.

"What could be more wonderful?" he repeated sarcastically. "To be with you all the time!"

"We both have work to do," she reminded him. "Then we can play."

"Some of us confuse the two when their work is like play."

She narrowed her eyes playfully. "Are you insinuating that I don't work hard?"

He shrugged. "I would never say that. But walking around looking pretty isn't a bad way to make a living."

"What?" She gasped. "There's more to it than that!"

"Yes," he acknowledged. "There's all that dieting."

"Well, it sure beats the hell out of those two-martini lunches you executives seem to prefer! Anyway, how can sitting through all those boring meetings be called work?"

He grinned. "You've got me, Lisle. Are we going to spend our remaining minutes together sparring?"

"It's up to you. I'll spar if that's what you want."

"You know what I'd rather be doing!"

She touched the front of his shirt. "Me too," she whispered. "I'll miss you, too, Hal." Then she winked and squeezed his hands. "Bring your long johns and ski jacket to Aspen."

"Will you ski with me this time?"

"Of course."

He narrowed his eyes as he recalled her previous reluctance to ski. "I thought you didn't want to risk getting hurt."

"I'm ready to take the chance." She smiled, and her violet eyes crinkled at the corners.

"Take a chance with me, Lisle. Let yourself love."

"I am, Hal. You don't realize how much I'm risking. You just can't." She shook her head. "It's too soon for talk of love. Please, don't . . ." Once again those violet eyes pleaded with him not to destroy her fantasy.

They could hear his flight number being called over the loudspeaker.

"If I don't go now, that damned plane will take off, and I'll be stuck here in L.A. without you. I'll call you, Lisle. Expect it. I'm finished with this business of no communicating! And I'll see you in Aspen in three weeks." He kissed her quickly, then took off at a jog.

"See you . . ." She had spoken in a whisper and now raised a hand to wave. As she watched him weaving through the crowd, her overactive imagination took charge.

His long runner's legs stretched to cover the concourse, and his strong, athletic form moved easily. Hal could star in a running-through-airports commercial, except that his hair

114

was gray. Gray? What the hell was wrong with her? What difference did gray hair make? She was just as guilty of age discrimination as the rest of the world. In her eyes gray was beautiful! God! She'd worked so hard to convince people of that! Hal was a handsome gray-haired man. He was her Viking—strong, but gentle. And already, as he disappeared from her sight, she couldn't wait to hold him again.

"What, Mother? You're going again? With *that* man?"

"Inga, please understand," Lisle begged.

"Oh, I'm trying, Mother. In fact, I was all prepared to apologize for being so narrow-minded about your plans for the Thanksgiving holiday. After I had time to think about it, I realized that you deserved an occasional fling. You need your own life, even if it interferes with your family.

"I'll admit Craig and I were being selfish by objecting. We simply wanted our mother with us over the holidays. And I know that you deserve to do what you want, Mother. But Christmas—that's the ultimate holiday! How could you leave then? It's such a joyous family time. You have grandchildren now, you know!"

Lisle felt weighted down with a hundred pounds of guilt. If she hadn't already chastised herself for having arranged to meet her lover during Christmas, Inga was there to do the job for her. Lisle had known it would be tough to confront her family, but she hadn't realized how tough. Was it too selfish of her and Hal to use the convenience of the Christmas holidays for their rendezvous? Should she leave her two grandchildren at Christmas? *They'll only be this age once!* Oh, how could she be so heartless?

"Actually, we didn't think the holidays would cause a problem, Inga. We chose Christmas because it would give us more time off from work, not because we wanted to miss family events." Lisle began gingerly to feel her way through an explanation. If she wasn't careful, she would change her own mind. "You know, I have that photo layout scheduled

115

for December twenty-first in Aspen, and it seemed logical for us to stay on for a few days."

"But through Christmas?" Inga repeated with dramatic exasperation.

"Yes." Lisle nodded meekly. For once, she wished Hal were standing here between them so he could explain it all to Inga. She needed strength right now, and Hal had plenty of it, enough for both of them. He would help her. Maybe she should call him. . . .

"I had even considered going to Aspen with you, Mother, remember? I have the time off and—"

Lisle's head snapped up. So *that* was what was behind Inga's anger! It had nothing to do with a grandmother's enjoyment of children and grandchildren at Christmastime, or with Lisle's own personal happiness! She could see it all clearly now. Inga expected to go to Aspen with her mother. Why hadn't she realized it before? She vaguely remembered discussing it briefly, when she had first received notice of the assignment.

Granted, Inga needed a vacation, for the divorce had left her depressed and bitter. Between little Alex and her job, there was no time or energy left for a social life. But must Lisle feel responsible for her daughter's resocialization? What about her own life?

Could it be that the only one who really cared about her happiness was Hal? How could he care so much about her, so soon?

Inga's tone was dramatic. ". . . of course, Mother, I know we had no set plans, but—"

Lisle decided to gamble. "Why, yes, we did mention you and Alex going along if you had the time off from work, Inga. Well, you still can go. I don't mind." Lisle smiled placidly, thinking how awkward it would be if Inga accepted her offer! What would Hal say . . . after going through the roof?

116

"And stay in the same room with you and what's-his-name? No, thanks!" Inga scoffed.

"Well, no, darling." Lisle spoke carefully. "You and Alex could stay in a room nearby."

"No, Mother." Inga shook her head firmly. "I can't afford a separate room."

"Don't worry about the money, Inga. I'll take care of the bill. It can be my Christmas present to you," Lisle said kindly.

"No, thank you. I have no intention of showing up as chaperone for my own mother! Anyway, I don't want to be away from my home and family during Christmas." She emphasized the "I" as if those who dared to be away during Christmas were wreckers of the blessed family.

"I can understand your not wanting to go under the present circumstances, Inga. I'm terribly sorry."

Lisle was wearing her hundred-pound guilt again. She knew that Hal would raise hell over this. Just why was she feeling sorry? Because Inga wasn't going? Hardly! She was relieved. Was she sorry because she would undoubtedly have a wonderful Christmas week with Hal? No! She couldn't wait to see him. Should she be sorry for having fun? Hell, no! She wouldn't feel guilty for wanting her own life simply because it meant spending the holiday away from her children and their families.

Lisle knew exactly what Hal would say. *To hell with the world! Let's go have fun, m'lady! We'll do anything your imagination dreams up!*

Lisle paced the floor. She knew her family loved her. Of that, she was sure. But she was not the center of their lives anymore. They had successful careers, friends, and families of their own to provide richness and fulfillment. So why should they be the center of her life as they once were?

Now she had Hal to provide some of the fulfillment missing from her life for so many years. And he wasn't interested in her pies or how she cooked the turkey. Nor did he care

117

where or when they met. Not really. He only wanted to spend time with her. To see her happy. He really didn't give a damn that they were spending Christmas Day together. That particular time had been chosen arbitrarily. He only wanted to be with her for as long as possible and was willing to fly from Delaware to Colorado to do just that.

Truthfully, Lisle could hardly wait to be with him. If it didn't happen at Christmas, they would have to wait another month or more before they could have another rendezvous. Another month without Hal would be awful.

Suddenly she smiled. "Inga, be sure to take lots of pictures of the kids Christmas morning because Grandma is going skiing!"

Inga rolled her eyes and mumbled scornfully, "Just wait till Craig hears about this!"

Lisle folded her arms and looked steadily at her daughter. "You know something, Inga? I don't give a damn what my son says!"

"Mother!"

But Lisle had already turned away from her protesting daughter. She had a lot to do to get ready for her ski trip with Hal.

Hal's footsteps crunched on the snow-packed sidewalk. Clean, cold Colorado air hit him full blast, and he inhaled deeply. He held his luggage and eyed the teeming Alpine village. Aspen always exuded a certain European flavor, and at this time of year the holiday spirit was strong. He paused to catch the distant jingling of bells, probably some couple was taking a sleigh ride across the snowy fields.

Lisle would say, *How romantic! Let's take a sleigh ride, Hal!* Oh, yes, this woman had definitely influenced his life. Even his thinking! Romantic, indeed! Still his heart quickened at the thought of her.

He would be seeing her soon. His lovely Lisle was somewhere in this tiny town right now! Hurrying up the steps at

118

the entrance to the lodge, he wondered if she would be waiting for him this time. Eagerly? With open arms? He recalled how she had clung to him at the Los Angeles Airport last month. On the phone she seemed as anxious to make this trip as he. She had called to say she would leave a message at the desk so he could go straight to their room. *Their* room! He tramped inside the lobby and asked briskly for any messages.

Hal's eyes scanned the note written in Lisle's precise handwriting. Poor visibility had delayed their work, and they were still shooting the magazine layout. She gave him the general location so that Hal could come out to the site and watch them work if he wanted. *If!* God! He could hardly wait to see her! To hold her!

He bounded up the stairs and unlocked the door to *their room.* It was semidark, but as he glanced around, he could tell Lisle had been there. The place was neat to a fault, and the scent of her favorite perfume lingered in the air, the traces just strong enough to drive him crazy! Hal dumped his luggage and raced down the narrow stairs, intent on finding Lisle.

The noise drew his attention, even before he could see the array of lights and the small crew of photographers and models.

A male voice could be heard, demanding and hard. "Smile, Lisle! Throw your head back a little. Smile, damn it! Pretend you're having fun!" He barked each emotion he wanted, and there was an urgency to his tone.

"It's hard to have fun when you're freezing," Lisle grated through smiling, blue-tinged lips.

"Her hair's wet! Hide it with that cossack hat!"

Hal stared, unbelieving, at the scene before him. He skirted the few observers until he stood at the inner edge of the circle.

Lisle, clad in full-length deep purple leotards, bright pink knitted leg warmers, and a short silver-fox coat, sprawled

119

sexily in the snow. Someone rushed forward and plopped a furry cossack hat on her head. Attendants hovered around her, moving in and out of camera range, while the photographer snapped like a madman and the director issued orders to everyone in a nonstop drone.

Responding to the barking demands, Lisle writhed in the snow. She lounged sensuously, kicked out both legs at the same time, then kicked one leg at a time. On command, she threw her head back, laughing gaily. *She should get an Oscar for best actress,* Hal thought wretchedly. *If one couldn't see the bluish color of her skin, one would think she was loving every minute.* But Hal knew Lisle was suffering, and it angered him to see her like this. Whatever made him think her work was easy?

She was wet and cold and . . . Damn! He couldn't believe his eyes! Lisle kicked a leg high in the air and her bare foot glared against the sparkling snow! *Barefooted!* How the hell could they ask her to do such a thing? If they really cared . . . He looked around and saw that the other models stood by waiting in similar attire. Red, blue, and black leotards shivered beneath fur coats and jackets in an array of colors. What a crazy idea! So this was the glamorous world of high fashion?

Hal bit back the expletives that perched on the tip of his tongue, only because he might embarrass Lisle, and probably prolong her suffering. So he stuffed cold hands in his pockets, braced himself against the chilling mountain wind that whipped around them, and glared angrily. It was a damn stupid way to make a living, and he would tell her so! Fortunately she couldn't see him, for the scowl on his face would have told her his thoughts.

"That hat won't work! Hides too much! I want the gray to show next to that coat!" The stern voice was giving directions again. "Get the hand dryer and dry her hair!"

Lisle sat patiently in the snow while someone blew her hair around, then brushed it quickly into shape. There followed more barked orders and still more shots. With attendants scurrying about her, Lisle was helped into another coat, this time an ankle-length white mink. She looked elegant as she drew it to her chin and swept about in the snow.

Then the session went from the urbane to the absurd. They whisked the white mink away and wound a long furry boa around her colorful leotards. It was rather like a strange snake wrapped around a purple popsicle!

"Okay, now everyone together! Then we're finished!"

Attractive young women in furs and brightly colored leotards appeared around Lisle to pose in various postures. They presented a spectacular display of beautiful women and expensive fur coats amid wild splashes of color in the snow. Yes, Hal had to admit, it was dramatic. These women's photos would probably appear in a national magazine, touched up so you couldn't see their blue lips, of course!

Finally the longed-for shout: "Okay, we're finished!"

The women scattered. Lisle was met on the sidelines by Hal's warm, open arms. There was no time for shy greetings, nor were there any sweet, affectionate words of longing, or eager smiles. The two of them were simply propelled into each other's arms. Their time together held too great an urgency, and they both knew it.

Lisle said nothing; it was as if she had expected him to be there to take care of her. It was as if no time had elapsed since their last meeting, as if no thousands of miles separated their lives. She clung to him, shivering, and Hal immediately stripped off his overcoat and wrapped her in it. He helped her into warm boots and whisked her off toward the lodge, murmuring his disapproval in barely audible expletives.

"I've changed my mind about your job, Lisle. It isn't easy."

She smiled with faint triumph.

Hal bared his teeth. "It's damned idiotic! How could you let those fools do this to you?"

Inside their room he jerked the bedspread back and

121

grabbed the insulated blanket. Lisle stood submissively still while Hal wrapped her in it and lifted her gently into the bed. "You wait right here while I run the bathwater."

"Where would I go?" she muttered through chattering teeth. "I'm frozen!"

"That's the damned truth! Crazy job you have, lady!"

Lisle nodded meekly. At the moment, with her teeth clacking together like clamshells, she had to agree. She couldn't remember ever being so cold, and even in the blanket she couldn't stop her arms and legs from shaking. What a way to greet your lover! She wanted to tell him how she'd missed him and how glad she was that he was here to take care of her. But she couldn't speak. She could hardly think straight!

She was vaguely aware of Hal's voice speaking into the phone. "Warm brandy and more blankets." He turned on the tap to fill the tub, then sat beside her and unwrapped the upper part of the blanket.

"No, don't!" she objected, suddenly jerking to life and grabbing for the blanket.

"Lisle," he said patiently. "I have to remove your wet clothes. Now, how do we get this thing off?" He gazed helplessly for a moment at the one-piece leotard that covered her torso.

"It comes off from here," she explained, pulling her arms free. "It's stretchy."

"Oh." He helped her ease out of the wet garment, his hands grazing the sides of her bare breasts and hips as he peeled it away. He threw it in a corner. "I know this is a dumb question from an absolute greenhorn—I don't understand a thing about this crazy business you're in—but why in hell were you lying in the snow with practically no clothes on—and barefooted!" He pulled off her soggy leg warmers and tossed them in the growing heap.

"At this moment I'm not sure I can explain, Hal," Lisle muttered through chattering teeth. "Our director is always

122

looking for innovative shots. He'll have us climbing on playground equipment in fabulous evening attire, playing in autumn leaves dressed in wild-animal-print lingerie, or making angels in the snow in fur coats and leotards. Anything that gets attention and looks like fun." She lifted her hips while Hal tugged on her tights. "He called us his angels in the snow," she said, chuckling ruefully.

Hal's hands encased her icy feet as he tried to keep his anger under control. "The man's insane! Barefooted, for God's sakes! All of you were cold and wet! You'll probably have pneumonia from this kind of exposure! You want to know my opinion? You looked more like wretched ragamuffins than angels!"

"No one asked your opinion," Lisle told him unkindly.

He ignored her comment and tucked the blanket back around her shivering nude body. "Anytime you do anything so stupid, you're going to hear from me."

Lisle's hands crossed automatically to her arms, and she rubbed them briskly. "Oh, Hal, you're probably right. I'm so cold . . ."

"I know you are, baby," he said as he held her tightly in his arms. "Ah, Lisle, love, I hate to see you suffering like this for a goddamn job. My sweet, sweet baby." His hands traveled the length of her, moving constantly over the blanket to help warm her chilled body.

She pressed her face gratefully to his chest, trying to absorb his warmth. It was so good to have Hal here with her. To have someone who cared just for her; someone to take care of her and love her. "Oh, Hal," she wailed. "I'm so miserable. Maybe I'm too old for this job. Too old for everything."

Hal held her away from him and looked into her eyes. "Oh, no, you aren't. You aren't too old for anything you want to do. But, my God, Lisle! This is crazy! No one can spend hours practically nude in cold, wet snow and not feel miserable! Your director is an idiot!" He paused, and they could hear water gushing. "Oh, damn! I forgot the tub—"

He dashed into the bathroom and cut off the water, then returned to rummage through her makeup case. "Now, where's that thing that holds up your hair? Ah, here it is." He pushed her damp curls behind her ears, then twisted her hair into a clumsy knot at the back of her head and secured it with the large clasp he'd seen her use on occasion. His fingers gently stroked the ragged tendrils away from her face and up off her neck. He caressed her face and kissed it repeatedly as he worked. "No reason for your hair to get any wetter than it already is. Now, you need hot water. Come on, love."

He steered her into the steamy room and removed the damp blanket from her shoulders. With gentle, helping hands he eased her into the tub of hot water. The steam rose as the water swelled around her, eventually covering her slender form up to the neck.

"Oooo, Hal, this is heavenly. I'm so glad you're here." Her eyes closed, and Lisle lay perfectly still, as if in a stupor. The water, with encouragement from Hal's hands, began to work its soothing, healing magic, and slowly but surely a small fire began to burn at the heart of her being.

Through the steam Hal handed her a glass containing a hot drink. "Drink this," he ordered gently. "And when you're finished, there's more."

She accepted the glass without question and sipped obediently. She didn't care about the calories in the drink, or even what kind of mixture it was. After all, Hal was in charge, and that was a nice feeling.

Hal knelt beside the tub and dipped his hands into the foamy water to stroke and massage every numbed part of her body. He rubbed her shoulders and arms vigorously until a tingling sensation started to spread through them. He caressed the full length of her, moving from her breasts, to her hips, and down her long legs to her icy feet. Soon she

124

was afire with his touch, and still he continued, slipping his hands under her to knead her buttocks and slick back. She sighed contentedly. His touch was wonderful.

By the time Lisle had drunk two glasses of the hot toddy, she was feeling warm and totally relaxed. Hal helped her out of the tub and toweled her off briskly, not allowing her to do anything but brush her teeth.

"Now sit," he directed, "while I dry your hair." Aiming a hair dryer at the wet strands of her dark hair, Hal went about it with a well-meaning clumsiness. "Now this." Once again his hands covered her body, this time in applying a warm, smooth emollient cream. He rubbed each limb carefully. When she was about as limp as a rag doll, he tucked her in bed.

Lisle floated into a dreamworld where Hal was the strong Viking who carried her through the snow to his warm castle. She was vaguely aware of the Viking's nude body folding her to him, providing heat and security throughout the night. To keep him from escaping at dawn, Lisle wrapped her arms about his chest, molding her body to his, clinging as if she would never let go. "Hal. Hal . . . hold me. Keep me warm. I need you . . ."

Throughout the long hours of the night he held her gently —pressing soft femininity against chiseled masculinity—and with a restrained passion. He watched the frown on her sleeping face change to a contented smile. Over and over he recalled her mumbled plea: *"Hold me . . . I need you."*

Morning came, and Lisle awakened rested and warm in Hal's arms. His body snuggled against her back, and she basked in the heat that radiates quite naturally between two nude bodies. It was sooo comfortable just to lie there, enjoying the feel of his form against hers. Slowly, surely, in the morning stillness, an incipient passion kindled. It was a gradual process, barely detectable at first. Only the most sensitive being would notice. Eventually, though, the tiny fire became a blaze that inflamed them both.

125

Lisle stirred first, pressing erotically against him. Caught in the circle of his arms, she turned to face him.

"Hi." She smiled sleepily.

"Morning, m'lady." He greeted her with a grin. "How are you feeling?"

"Warm," she answered shyly. "Very warm . . ."

"Good. That means I did my job well." His hand brushed her cheek and pushed her hair back. "I'm in charge now, Lisle. It's hot soup, hot toddies, and bed all day."

"I especially like the bed part," she murmured. "With you."

"I'll do my best to keep you warm and content."

She squirmed against him. "Content, like this?"

"Hmmmm, very nice." His hands caressed her bare back and pressed her hips.

"Hal," she murmured, her lips close to his. "Thank you for taking such good care of me last night. I know that was a miserable way to greet your lover. I'm sorry to have been such a dud—"

"Nonsense," he said gruffly. "I'm glad I was here to take care of you, Lisle."

"What would I have done without you, Hal? You were very good to me."

"Don't you know by now, Lisle, that I care for you? Deeply." His lips came to hers, brushing against them softly at first, persuading and gentle. His tongue lightly tingled the edges of her lips, and she quivered with desire. Following a trail down the column of her neck, his kisses came to rest on a bare creamy breast. With intimate finesse he brought each nipple to pink-tinged sharpness, knitting them between tongue and lip until she moaned in sweet torture.

He pressed his hand between her legs, and she fell back, inviting him to carry on. "Oh, Hal, yes. Love me . . ." She breathed shakily in anticipation. His gentle strokes gradually grew in intensity until she thrust hard against him.

He lifted his chest tightly against hers, pressing her

breasts flat. His waist rubbed against hers, and his legs spread between hers, his masculinity teasing her. "I do love . . ."

She reached for him, stroking intimately until his fevered rasp stopped her.

"Lisle, easy—"

The sharpness of his voice caused her to jerk her hands away. She let them rest shamelessly on his thighs, continuing her maddening stroking. "Hal, please . . . you're driving me crazy! Please, come on—"

His lips crushed her in sweet union, pausing, caressing. Gradually his tongue slid between her lips and teeth, seeking warm gratification. At the same time his firmly aroused body entered hers, deliberately and, oh, God, slowly! Ever so slowly!

She gasped and opened her lips wide in silent entreaty: *Please, God, let him increase the pace.* But he still moved deliberately. Touching her tongue to his, warm velvet to warm velvet, she arched and writhed and moaned her sweet agony. Still he continued his leisurely exploration, obviously enjoying each merciless moment.

Finally! With an engulfing thrust they were joined! Just when she thought their union was complete, he moved and the agony started again!

"Damn it, Hal!"

"Yes, m'lady?"

"Don't tease me like that! Please, don't . . ." She moaned against his shoulder, digging her teeth into the tough flesh that stretched across his muscles.

"Do you need me, Lisle? Tell me what you need!" he demanded.

"Yes! I . . . need you . . . Hal. Please, don't stop."

At last, abandoning all restraint, Hal filled her with the full force of his love. "I love you, Lisle. I want to love you completely."

"Yes," she murmured, hardly understanding his words as her fingers dug fiercely into his buttocks.

She was only aware of the intensity of the moment; of the almost violent eruption of passion as together, in the ultimate union of man and woman, they reached the height of ecstasy. He called her name, ardently, lovingly. Then all was quiet, and they held each other, as if clinging to the satisfaction they had shared.

Lisle spent the entire day submitting to Hal's hovering ministrations. She willingly followed his orders to sip hot soup, hot tea, and, by evening, hot toddy. She wasn't exactly sick, but he convinced her this was essential preventive treatment. In quiet moments Hal even joined her in bed. At her suggestion they read aloud parts of her historical novel and made love again. . . .

Though unaccustomed to the relative inactivity, Lisle was quite happy to remain in the room the entire day. She did not object when Hal insisted on waiting on her, hand and foot. He even gave her a warm shower and washed and dried her hair. She was malleable clay in his hands, desiring nothing more than to be cared for and loved. The next morning they slept late.

"Laziness is habit-forming, you know." She smiled and stroked his back.

"Hope so." He dipped his head to kiss her breast. "I'd like nothing better than to make love to you every day for the rest of my life."

"Which would be about a week, at your present pace!" She laughed.

"Ah, but I'd die sublimely happy!"

"Well, I would feel extremely guilty. Frankly, I'd rather have you around a little longer than that."

"They say lovers live longer. I'd like that to be us, Lisle. Together for the rest of our lives."

"We are. We're lovers already, Hal."

"But I want us to be together all the time."

"You know that's impossible," she said nervously. "Our lives are too complicated."

"Nothing is too complicated if you want it badly enough. And I want you very badly. We could simplify things, Lisle."

"Hal, don't . . ."

"To show you how serious I am, I've put my house on the market."

"What? Hal . . . why?" She didn't really want to know why—was even afraid to know why—but the word had just popped out.

His voice was low and very serious. "You know I don't want to risk losing you, Lisle. I want you to marry me."

CHAPTER EIGHT

Lisle wrenched herself away from him and sat on the edge of the bed, holding her head in her hands. Anguish tore through her body. Feeling very much as if she'd been kicked in the stomach, she rasped, "I can't, Hal. You know I can't."

He responded with remarkable calm, perhaps as self-protection. "No. I'm not convinced that you *can't*. Won't, maybe."

She shook her head vigorously. Her sable shoulder-length hair with its silver streak fell around her face. Still Lisle refused to look up at him, sensing the set of his features at that moment: the chiseled chin held firmly; the lips a taut, thin line. Blue eyes fierce and . . . wounded. Oh, God—she couldn't bear that. To see him hurt, and to know she had caused the pain, was pure agony.

"You don't understand," she whispered, then raised her head slightly. "My life, my career, my family, are stable just the way they are now. But they—they complicate the issue for us, Hal. It isn't easy to consider taking a husband at my age. After all this time. . . ."

Lisle heard the rustling of the sheets as Hal got out of the bed. Her heart twisted inside her breast, for she knew he was thinking *An affair is fine, but marriage is strife!* Oh, God—it shouldn't be that way at all! But she was so scared of it!

Suddenly Lisle realized that what they had been doing was wrong. Wrong because she didn't want to get married. Wrong because it gave each of them false illusions of love

130

and happiness. Maybe they needed more time for their love to develop, to grow from a fantasy into the real thing. Obviously she needed more time.

"And for me," Hal was saying as he dressed, "it isn't easy to agree to take a wife, after all these years. But, Lisle, it goes beyond what's easy. It has to do with caring—and loving. Can't you tell how much I love you?"

She met his gaze sadly, at last. "I care for you, too, Hal. But to say I loved you that deeply—" How could she tell him her true feelings without hurting him more?

He reached a gentle finger under her chin and caressed her cheek. "I find being with you a joy, Lisle. I'm willing to give up anything—everything—for that privilege. Apparently you don't feel the same."

His words, like a knife, dug deep inside her. To deny his statement would be to make a commitment she wasn't prepared to give. To agree would be to reject everything they meant to each other. Oh, God, she didn't know what she felt right now, except that she didn't want their relationship to end. Not yet. Not like this. But could they go on like this? She was afraid to ask.

The silence stretched between them, widening the gap that separated them. Then Hal smiled wryly, sadly. "Actually, we've only been with each other about three weeks, yet I feel as though I've known you forever. In my opinion, our relationship has developed into something very special. If you need more time to realize this, Lisle, I can wait." He grabbed a coat and walked out of the room.

"Hal?" She gasped. "Where are you going?"

Only the echo of his receding footsteps answered her.

Lisle scrambled to dress and hurried outside into the snow-covered village of Aspen. She walked up one street and down another, wondering where Hal would go at a time like this. Skiing? No, he hadn't dressed for it. Maybe he went for a bite of breakfast, since they hadn't eaten. She finally found him in a tiny coffeehouse and slid eagerly onto the bench beside him, close enough to feel the invigorating warmth of his thigh. Slowly he turned, his loving, pain-filled eyes on her.

"Hal, please don't do this to us. Why can't we stay the same?" she asked breathlessly, squeezing her cold hands together.

"Is that what you want?"

She nodded and smiled hopefully.

His hand encased hers on the table. "Still living out your fantasies, Lisle?"

"What's wrong with staying the way we are, Hal? Must we always be so serious?"

"No." He sighed. "Not always."

"Don't ruin it for us, Hal. This is the way I want it."

"Lisle . . ."

"How about sharing your hot chocolate?"

"You're an unusual woman, Lisle. I just can't figure you out." He pushed the mug toward her.

"Don't try." She wrapped cold fingers around the warm mug and drank from it gratefully. "I tried to tell you at the beginning, but things got out of hand. It'll be better, Hal, just to stay the way we are."

Hal clenched his jaws but didn't answer.

They ordered more hot chocolate and ate a strange breakfast of whole wheat toast and slices of cheese and apples. They talked, careful to avoid serious matters. Eventually light laughter could be heard in their little booth, and Hal and Lisle seemed to be the same joyful couple as before. However, an avowal of love always changes things, tints feelings. Laughter masked the seriousness of the moment.

After brunch they bought tickets for the afternoon ski lift and skied until dusk. At dinner, later that evening, Lisle forgot her usual obsession with calories, having worked up a healthy appetite on the slopes, and joined Hal in wolfing down a huge steak dinner. They finished off a bottle of wine, then disappeared into their upstairs hideaway, where they made mad, passionate love.

It became a pattern. They slept late every day, wandered about the quaint village hand in hand, and ended up at the little coffeehouse for hot chocolate and whatever savory items they wanted for brunch. It was a little wacky, but fun, doing whatever they wanted to do. Then they skied until dark, returning weak-kneed and exhausted. Following a whopper of a dinner they fell into each other's arms, sometimes massaging aching muscles and not always making love. It was very comfortable.

They woke on Christmas Day to the sound of "Jingle Bells."

"Merry Christmas," he murmured, kissing her forehead and eyelids and cheeks.

Lisle snuggled closer, thoroughly enjoying the attention. "Merry Christmas. This is the warmest Christmas morning I've had in years."

"It's going to get even warmer if you don't stop that," he threatened.

Her eyes popped open. "But I have a present for you first!" She leapt out of bed and began to scramble about the room.

"What in hell are you doing?"

"Fixing the Christmas tree. There!" She snapped on the tall lamp on the dresser and draped it with a green scarf. "With a little imagination, *voilà!* a Christmas tree!"

He laced his fingers behind his head and watched her antics. "Well, God knows, you have enough imagination for that! Here we are in Christmas-tree country, surrounded by at least a million of them, and I have to pretend with a lamp and scarf!"

"Oh, hush complaining!" She approached him, holding out an oblong gift. "If you aren't careful with your sharp tongue, I'll sing 'Jingle Bells.' And believe me, that would be sheer torture!"

"How about 'Over the Hills and Through the Woods to Grandmother's House We Go'?" He chuckled devilishly.

Her violet eyes flashed tiny purple daggers. "How would you like to receive your Christmas gift—cracked over your head?"

"Easy now, m'lady, it's just a joke!" He laughed.

"Well, it isn't funny! Here." She thrust the package into his hands. "Before I do something I'll later regret!"

He tore into the gift and pulled out a bottle of Canadian white Riesling.

"To remind us of that first night we spent together." She smiled and produced two plastic goblets and a corkscrew.

He kissed her gently. "Lisle, what a romantic thing to do. Where did you get this? I don't think you can buy it here."

She gave him a sly smile. "Don't forget, I have friends who travel."

"Well, it was an excellent idea. Shall we imbibe?" He uncorked the bottle and filled their glasses. "Here, this should give the ol' taste buds a workout this morning. To us, Lisle. . . ."

"To us, Hal. . . ."

"Now, your gift." He rummaged in his suitcase until he finally found the small present.

Lisle gaped at the tiny jewelry box, and her heart sank. Surely he didn't have an engagement ring for her! With nervous fingers she slowly opened it. "What—what is it?" She lifted a delicate gold chain with a tiny gold object attached. "A ship?"

"A Viking ship, m'lady. Wear it and remember that I will follow you to the ends of the earth."

"Oh, Hal, it's beautiful. Thank you. Here, put it on me."

He fastened the shiny golden chain around her neck, and it glistened against her otherwise nude body. "Beautiful."

She wrapped her arms around his shoulders and pressed the Viking ship to his chest. "What a wonderful Christmas, Hal."

As they descended to the bed, he murmured, "I think it's getting warmer in here."

"A veritable inferno. . . ." She laughed and pulled him over her.

Later they took a sleigh ride, loudly singing "Jingle Bells" and every other song that popped into their heads. Neither of them mentioned Hal's proposal. In fact, that early, serious conversation was not touched on again. They pretended it had never happened—almost believed that it hadn't. But it was there, simmering.

Christmas night was quiet, the clamor of the holiday week having disappeared. A peaceful glow settled over the town as most of the Christmas crowd cleared out, leaving Hal and Lisle in relative privacy in their secluded Alpine village. They, too, would have to leave the next day. In the little coffeehouse they sipped coffee laced with Kahlua and topped with a dollop of whipped cream. The flickering firelight cast weird shadows on the pine-paneled walls, and a golden glow suffused their faces.

"You look tired." Hal smiled.

"Um-hum," she agreed. "Even with all I've been eating—" She gestured to the heaping mug between her hands. "—and drinking, I don't think I've put on an ounce."

"Skiing is a vigorous sport."

She smiled devilishly. "So is loving."

He shrugged, palms out in concession. "What can I say?"

"You could say you're tired too!" She leaned her face against his sleeve and clung to his arm. "You know, Hal, this has been the best time we've had together. The best one yet."

They were quiet for a moment, deep in reminiscence. No one mentioned that mutual caring and growing love could be the reason for this being their best time together yet. That would have been an admission.

Hal's eyes grew serious. "I like to think the best is yet to come for us. That reminds me. Where to next, m'lady?

135

What's your pleasure? A big city . . . towering mountains . . . a distant shore . . . a deserted island?"

She looked up curiously. "Do you have a deserted island in mind, sir? That sounds very appealing."

He pursed his lips, thinking. "No, but if that's your heart's desire, I could sure as hell come up with one soon enough!"

"I'm tentatively scheduled to do a layout in Cancun sometime in February. How does that sound?"

"Cancun? Perfect! Not quite an island, but a peninsula will do."

"It isn't too far to travel to from Delaware?"

"Foolish girl! Nothing is too far away, if I can be with you!"

"That's what I like about you, Hal! You're eager for fun and adventure, anywhere!"

He lifted her hand to his lips, caressing the knuckles, then turned it over to kiss the palm. "What I like about you, Lisle"—he paused, then finished softly—"is everything."

"Hal—"

"I love you, Lisle. Maybe someday you'll love me too."

"But, I—"

"Until then, we can be friends or lovers or whatever you imagine for us in that crazy, pretty head of yours."

She smiled faintly. By interrupting her reply, he had relieved her of having to declare—or deny—love. "I imagine us as lovers on a deserted beach in Cancun in February."

"So be it," he swore solemnly, and then kissed her again, this time with persuasive lips that softly parted hers. They had so little time left to be together in the Alpine hideaway, and they hurried back to their room to make good use of the precious moments until it was time to leave.

"What does a daughter know? Only that I know my own mother pretty well and lately you've been acting very strangely." Inga followed Lisle into the living-room.

136

"I've been under a little pressure at work." Lisle began to squirt the leaves of a rubber tree with unnecessary vigor. This was what she liked. Watering the silent plants. They didn't ask questions, or demand explanations for unreliable behavior, or clamor for vows of love. They were grateful enough for the watering.

"Does that explain your slightly erratic behavior, Mother? Not returning my calls? Forgetting when you promised to come over to my house? I can overlook it, but poor little Alex was so disappointed that his grandmother didn't do what she said she would do!"

Lisle cast her daughter a cold, steely glance. Poor little Alex? Damn, Inga was laying it on thick. "Sorry about that, Inga. I—I'll explain to Alex, if I ever get over this guilt trip you're loading on me. He's young, though. He'll forget about my rudeness—that is, if you'll let him."

"If *I* let him?" Inga huffed indignantly. "I don't have to remind him. Children have remarkable memories when it comes to being disappointed."

"Well, mine certainly do!"

Inga folded her arms. "Do you realize it's been weeks since we were all together for Sunday supper?"

"Oh?" Lisle paused, then decided quickly to emend the situation. "Okay, we'll have Sunday supper this week." Maybe that would appease her irate family. But concern for their feelings was by no means the only source of stress in her life. Work seemed to be a continuous battle. For every two steps forward in her fight for fairness, she was knocked back three. Oh, how she wished a simple dinner would solve everything—her problems with the kids, the job, even Hal.

Oh, Hal. Her heart wrenched at the thought of him. She remembered how she'd left him the day after Christmas. His face was tight, his smile forced. And his eyes . . . the hurt in them. God, he had looked wretched! And it was all her fault. All! She bore that guilt heavily, too, but hadn't talked to anyone about it.

137

"Mother—"

"Yes?" Lisle jerked herself back to reality. "Yes, Inga?"

"Mother, listen to me! I'll bring a couple of pies." Inga's voice held a certain pride. "Since, uh, Thanksgiving, I've found that I can whip up a pretty fair pumpkin pie. And if Veronica will bring a casserole, you won't have to do a thing. Just provide drinks. Coffee or tea is fine. How does that sound?"

"Great," Lisle said without enthusiasm. "Just great."

While Inga babbled on, happy at last with the promise of a family gathering, Lisle could think only of Hal and that she must call him—that night. She had to change their plans. And she needed to talk to him, needed someone who cared. What would happen if she just dropped everything and caught a plane that night for Delaware? The idea was, of course, preposterous, completely irrational, but what she needed tonight was to be wrapped in Hal's strong arms. He would take care of everything. . . ."

She emptied the squirt bottle on the bushy asparagus fern, vaguely aware that she had dribbled water on the floor. She grabbed a towel from the bathroom in the hall and slapped it over the small puddles, sliding it around with her feet.

"What's wrong at work, Mother?"

Lisle looked up, surprised. "What makes you say that?"

"You said you had pressures at work." Inga gave her mother a confused glance.

"Oh. That. Well, there are always pressures, you know. Just the usual problems one experiences when one works for someone else."

Inga watched her mother's jerky motions and wondered what else could be bothering her. "What about this man you keep meeting secretly? Is he causing any problems for you?"

Lisle whirled around. "Of course not! Anyway, that's none of your business, Inga!"

"Take it easy, Mother. I don't mean to pry. But I don't

138

want him causing you any trouble. It's only because I care about you, not because I want to interfere."

"Well, he isn't!"

"You just seem so uptight. Actually, you have been since Christmas, Mother. Did things go all right with you two in Aspen?"

"Yes. Everything's fine," Lisle muttered briskly.

"I wish you felt more comfortable about sharing your feelings with me. If you have a problem, Mother, it might help just to talk about it."

Lisle looked down at her hands. Inga was trying hard to be helpful—to be more than a daughter. But no one had the answers. Not Hal. Certainly not Lisle. Maybe Inga was right, though. Just talking about things sometimes helped.

"Inga, I—it's just that . . . Oh, this is so hard." Lisle sighed and sat on one of the rattan chairs.

Inga sat opposite her, quiet and serious.

Lisle twisted her fingers together nervously. "I lost an assignment at work." She blurted out the words.

"Why?"

"My age," she said bitterly.

"Oh, Mother," said Inga consolingly. "Which assignment?"

"The one to Cancun. I've been reassigned to do a spring display in Odessa. Odessa, Texas, for God's sake!"

Inga raised her eyebrows and spoke hopefully. "Odessa could be a good potential market. There's oil money in that little town."

"I know. It's just that . . ." Should she tell Inga? Then the words slipped out: "Hal and I were going to meet in Cancun!"

Inga made a silent O with her lips, and watched as her mother picked an invisible piece of lint off her slacks.

"And Craig doesn't help matters by raising hell over everything I do. He's insisting that I break off this affair or get married. He seems to have forgotten that he and Veronica lived together at one time!" Lisle knew that she was floundering about, seemingly unable to hit on the thing that troubled her most. "First the job, then Craig and you—"

Inga reached out quickly to embrace her mother's shoulders. "I'm sorry, Mother. I didn't realize we were being so hard on you. Don't let Craig's outbursts get to you. Your son just doesn't want to think of his mother as a sensual woman."

"And you do?" Lisle scoffed.

Inga chuckled bitterly. "No, I guess not. It isn't easy thinking of your mother making love to a man, especially a man we've never met. But I recognize that you're a woman who needs love and affection beyond what your children can offer. You're certainly mature enough to make your own decisions. Don't feel guilty because of us, Mother. Do whatever you think is best for you."

Lisle's eyes glistened with unshed tears. Perhaps Inga was seeing her as a woman with the fears and desires of any woman, not just as a mother who should find fulfillment in children and grandchildren alone. "I don't know what brought about this sudden change in you, Inga, but I appreciate your support. This whole thing hasn't been easy for me either."

"I know it has been difficult juggling work, children, and a demanding lover. Do you want to know what I really think of my mother's affair? Woman to woman?" There was a faint smile on her lips.

Lisle slumped against the back of her chair, expecting the worst. She had gotten it full force from her son. Why not from her daughter too? Perhaps Craig was right and she *was* behaving disgracefully for a fifty-one-year-old grandmother.

"I think it sounds . . . exciting. I'm delighted to know that you're flying all over the country to meet a man who apparently gives you a great deal of pleasure."

"What?" Lisle's chin dropped. Was she hearing her daughter right?

"Oh, some of it was hard for me to accept. And I'll admit to being extremely angry because you chose to go away over both major holidays. But on reflection, I realize that was just selfishness on my part. Even at Christmas. I was thinking of me, not you, Mother."

"I'm astounded, Inga. You've been so—"

"Negative?"

"Yes." Lisle smiled and let out a sigh of relief. So there was someone on her side, after all. Maybe it had helped to share her feelings with her daughter. They seemed closer; they were two women, not just mother and daughter.

"I can see that, now. I've been terribly unfair to you. Actually, I'm eager to meet this man who has swept my mother off her solid, independent feet! Tell me what he's like."

Lisle smiled, eager to talk about her lover, woman to woman. "Hal is a wonderful man. He's intelligent, handsome, fun. He's fifty-three years old." She paused and sighed. "Are we too old for this foolishness, Inga?"

"Of course not, Mother! You are still a young, sensitive woman, and it's only normal that you should have sexual feelings and emotions." Inga smiled warmly. "I must admit, I'm not surprised by this description of Hal. I'm sure he's quite a man for you to be so attracted to him."

"This whole thing has been like something out of a dream, just meeting the way we do," Lisle observed. She had the vague expression of a person who was trying to get her bearings in a fog.

"What does he do for a living?"

Lisle smiled patiently. She was talking to her daughter again. "He has his own management consulting firm in Wilmington, Delaware. Deals with business problems of major corporations."

"Does he have a family too?"

"No family. His wife died ten years ago. What is this,

141

Inga? You're putting me through the third degree just as my own mother would do!"

Inga rubbed her chin comically. "His own business, huh? Well, now, maybe he is good enough for my darling mother, after all."

"He also wants to marry me." Lisle halted, and she looked expectantly into her daughter's eyes.

"Mother." Inga spoke excitedly. "What a surprise! Are you—I mean, oh, dear. My mother. Married!"

Lisle shook her head vigorously and began to pace the floor. "You don't understand, Inga. I care for Hal but don't know if I want to marry him. I'm somewhat successful in my own right. And free. It's been a rather nice feeling all these years. So it's hard to think of relinquishing that hard-won freedom. I don't want to be dependent again. It's taken me years to learn to stand on my own two feet, and that isn't easily forfeited, even for love. Does any of this make sense? Am I crazy?"

Lisle listened in horror to her own words. What was she saying? That there was no room in her life for love? For Hal? How could she? He was the best thing to happen in her life in years, and here she was denying the beauty of his love. Chilled by her own thoughts, she hugged herself to still the anguish rising inside her.

Inga's voice was quiet. "Does he want you to give up your career and move to Delaware with him?"

Lisle shrugged. "We haven't actually discussed it. But I assume that's what he expects of me. Isn't that the way it usually works? The woman follows the man to the ends of the earth? Right now, Delaware seems like the end to me. Of my independence, anyway."

Although Lisle had revealed far more about Hal and their relationship than she had intended, she felt better afterwards. It seemed to bring her closer to Inga. Perhaps someday they could drop the inhibitions of the mother-daughter relationship. Then Inga would understand and accept Lisle

142

as she was, offering no judgments or unsolicited advice. Just sharing, one woman to another. She sighed, thinking maybe that was too idealistic.

Later that evening Lisle picked up the phone and called Hal. His voice thrilled her and made her wish even more that she could be close to him, wrapped in his arms that night.

"I—I have to change our plans, Hal. I'm not going to Cancun, after all. I lost the assignment."

"What happened, Lisle?"

She faked a laugh. "Lost it to a younger woman. They want models who look smashing in swimsuits. Someone decided plum-colored leotards and silver-fox furs were more my style."

He muttered a low but distinct "Damn!" then said, "Lisle, I don't know any woman who looks better in a swimsuit—or in nothing at all! They're a bunch of goddamn fools!"

"Hal, please. Don't humor me. That's the way it is in this business. I have to take my lumps. It's just—we can't : . ."

"To hell with Cancun! I just want to see you! Do you still want to go to a beach? Or can I meet you in Dallas?"

"No, not Dallas. Maybe Siberia!" She laughed bitterly. "I've been assigned to Odessa, Texas, instead of Cancun."

"Odessa? Where the hell is that?"

"A million miles from a beach."

"Don't worry. I'll find us a beach. What about Tampa?"

"Florida?" She blinked and tried to readjust her thinking.

"I have business in Tampa in a few weeks. Maybe we could even find some secluded beach house. The Gulf Coast is lovely this time of year."

"Oh. Okay. Sounds great." She wanted to sound pleased, but somehow Lisle couldn't muster up the usual eagerness she had when they spoke.

"It'll be terrific, Lisle. You'll see. Just being together is what we need, my love. I'll call you later about the date. We'll work something out, I promise."

"Hal . . ."

"Yes?"

"Hal, I miss you. Terribly."

He caught his breath, remembering that it had been three miserable weeks since they were last together. God, he ached to hold her. But he knew he had to wait for her. He had to give her time. "I miss you, too, my love."

CHAPTER NINE

The day Lisle landed at Tampa International the Florida skies were an astonishing blue and the sun shone with a blinding brilliance—just as the Florida Chamber of Commerce had promised in its campaign to lure a winter-bedeviled northern populace to the state. And now Lisle would have gladly given testimony of the beauty of Florida's Gulf Coast. Of course, with Hal to greet her, it could have been raining cats and dogs and she wouldn't have noticed.

The minute she hit the end of the concourse, Hal grabbed her and whirled her around. "We're going to have an adventure you won't soon forget! This is a fantasy come to life, staged just for us, Lisle! My God! You look great! And I've missed you like hell!"

"Hal—" She staggered at his enthusiastic greeting. "Hal, what are you talking about?"

"The Gasparilla Invasion! It's tomorrow!"

She pushed her hair behind one ear and blinked in confusion. "What in hell is the Gasparilla Invasion?" Was this her Hal? The reserved and conservative Hal who favored three-piece pinstripes?

He grabbed both her arms. "Pirates, my love! Real live pirates—a perfect fantasy for you!"

"What?" She laughed at his excitement as he ushered her along. "I don't believe you!"

"You'll see! And you'll love it, I guarantee. This is a yearly event. Pirates take over the whole city, just like they did two

145

hundred years ago. It'll be a week of parties and festivals and torchlight parades at midnight! And food—oh, God, the food!"

"Oh, great. That's just what I need. More calories! Hal, did you plan this?" She stood stock-still, trying to sort out the threads of his story.

"The Gasparilla Invasion?" A devilish smile crossed his face. "Yeah, my love. Staged the whole damn thing, just for you."

"I mean, did you bring me here at this time because you knew I was discouraged about the canceled job assignment? And you knew I'd love a pirate invasion of the city of Tampa?"

"See? You aren't the only one with a love of fantasy and fun. Tampa loves a pirate, just like you do! I want you to realize that everything exciting doesn't happen on the beaches of Cancun. We may even find a beach of our own in a little hidden cove. Stick with me, kid. I'll take ya places! Now, let me see a smile on those million-dollar lips."

"Oh, Hal." She smiled, unable to resist his delightful bantering.

"Come on, m'lady," he urged her impatiently, "let's get your luggage. I've found a beautiful old Spanish hotel that'll make you think you're in the land of strolling guitarists and flamenco dancers. That is, if you don't look past the courtyard. It's near Ybor City, home of the best black beans and yellow rice in the world."

"E-bore City?" She frowned, still puzzled.

He ushered her through the airport. "Ybor City. Y-B-O-R. It's Spanish, so the Y sounds like E. It's the Latin section of Tampa."

Before too long they were settled in a gorgeous old pink-stucco hotel with a red-tiled roof. A banana tree grew right by their window. They lunched in a tiny restaurant with an elaborate fountain in the courtyard. A separate café was reserved, as custom demanded, for those who enjoyed discussing politics over cups of strong Cuban coffee.

"I'm feeling very Spanish." Lisle moaned as she stared at the huge bowl of black beans and yellow rice topped with chopped onions and a dash of vinegar. She bit into a hunk of crusty Cuban bread. "You're a disastrous influence on me, Hal Kammerman! I always ruin my diet when I'm with you. I just can't say no. Look at all this food. Nothing on this table has less than a hundred calories per bite! And these raw onions! My breath will probably be rare for days!"

"To hell with calories! And as for your breath"—he leaned over and kissed her lips—"I love it!"

"It's a good thing you're eating onions too. That way, you can't complain! We'll both have dragon breath!" She laughed.

"Two dragons! Wouldn't have it any other way! What's good for you is good for me. Or is it the other way around?" He kissed her nose, then reached for the frosty carafe. "More sangria?"

She held her goblet out boldly. "Why not? What's a few hundred more calories?"

"We'll work them off, Lisle. I have some *very* special exercises in mind," he said seriously.

"I'll bet you have!"

"Jogging, my dear. Jogging!"

Later that afternoon they strolled through the Latin section of Tampa with its old-world architecture and boarded-up cigar factories. In the evening, they enjoyed paella and wine in the gracious candle-lit surroundings of the Columbia Restaurant. It was almost like being in Spain, with the sound of strumming guitars and lilting Spanish at every turn. That night they slept in each other's arms again, alone in their dreamworld.

The next day, more brilliant and sunny than the previous one (if that was possible), found them amid the cheering crowd watching the pirate invasion of the city. The colorful

Spanish armada—a full square-rigged pirate ship teeming with costumed sailors, accompanied by flag-bedecked boats of all sizes and types—sailed bravely into the Tampa Bay with cannons and guns blazing.

"Ye mystic krewe" of the wicked pirate ship *Gasparilla* conquered the city forthwith and set about providing fun and frolic for all their captives. Rather than staying for the full range of festivities, Lisle and Hal decided to search out a more private beach bungalow and crossed the Sunshine Skyway Bridge heading southward from Saint Petersburg.

When they drove past Bradenton, Hal turned to continue along Longboat Key, a small island that ran parallel to the mainland. They found a lovely stretch of secluded beach and decided to explore it.

"Did you bring your swimsuit?" he asked her before they were even out of the car.

"Yes." She nodded.

"Well, forget it. No one can see us here."

She was startled. "What? Are you saying we should swim in the nude?"

"Sure. It's the perfect place. And we've got perfect timing. Everyone with any sense of fun is involved in the invasion around the bay. The rest are working. That leaves us here all alone. Why bother with suits?"

"Well, because . . . what if someone comes up?"

He shrugged. "So?"

"Hal! You're absolutely decadent!" She laughed and began to pull furiously at her shirt and shorts.

He took her hand, and they ran, completely nude, to the nearest stretch of water. Frolicking in the warm gulf waters like a couple of dolphins, they forgot both the real and their make-believe worlds. They were the only ones alive, and they laughed and enjoyed each other to the fullest. Touching, kissing, and playing in the warm sun was the only reality they knew or cared about.

Hal lifted her in his arms and held her against his chest,

kissing her cheeks and lips and neck. "Ah, my love, you're sweet and wet and warm . . . and ripe for love!" He carried her to the water's edge and lowered her to the sand.

She smiled and dug her fingers into the muscles along his shoulders. "No one has called me ripe in many a year." She cooed laughingly.

"Aren't you? Ready for love?" His lips teased her earlobe and created a small ripple of sensual pleasure that grew in intensity with every succeeding touch.

"Ready for you," she whispered in a low, sexy voice, and allowed her hands to travel down his sides and hips and over the taut male buttocks. Then her curious fingers moved boldly to meet at his front.

"Lisle—" he rasped.

She closed her eyes and stroked him, enjoying the moment every bit as much as he was.

"Lisle—I'm going to explode if you don't stop this instant!"

She slipped her hands around his waist and pressed closer to him. "You won't tease me anymore, will you, Hal?"

"Is that a threat?"

"No more teasing?" she demanded, arching against his burgeoning flesh.

"Just loving," he promised as he bent to kiss the pert cherry buds on her breasts. The rays of the sun prickled her skin intimately, and when his lips touched her, a throbbing heat coursed through her bare body.

Delicately he kneaded her breasts, supple and glistening with moisture from their swim. His tongue lapped at errant drops of water that rolled down the sides of her breasts, then supped on her salty-tasting nipples. They became hard with desire as his tongue laved them—the purifying strokes transforming them into sweet morsels of delight. She moaned softly and pressed her throbbing breasts against his hands, begging silently for more.

149

"Is that nice?" His fingertips brushed over her glowing, moist skin.

"Hmmmm," she whispered, and closed her eyes.

Gentle masculine strokes fluttered over her ribs and waist to the downy juncture of her legs. His fingers spread through her curls, and she arched against the heel of his hand.

His hands gripped her thighs, separating them, gently seeking the sensitive silken flesh. She moved rhythmically with the swell of the tiny waves that now licked at their feet. His fingers stroked, caressed, and probed every part of her body, skillfully bringing her to the fevered edge of ecstasy. His fingers grazed over her firm, lustrous stomach, kindling a wild passion within them both. Her legs were pure moist silk as the tiny gulf waves lapped against them.

He slipped into her, and she whimpered, bowing uncontrollably against his hand. Then he reached around to cup her sandy buttocks and thrust her erotically against him. She rocked of her own accord and made sweet sounds of pleasure. Grasping his hips, she dug half-moons into his flesh as she pulled him into her.

Suddenly they were together, writhing, digging, plunging with the wildly cresting waves of passion that washed over them. The erotic waves resounded and surged, raging through them, building energy, finally swelling to a vertiginous peak. Then, amid cries of joy, their wave of passion crashed on the sandy shore. A glorious quiet settled over them while their hearts throbbed wildly in their heaving breasts. The primitive satisfaction gave way to a deeper relief, the fulfilled love of one for another. They collapsed in the sweet languor of their love until water from the rising tide curled around them, waking them to the real world.

"Hal . . ."

"I know." Hal shifted. "Let me wash you." They slid into the waist-deep water and lovingly splashed each other, exchanging cleansing caresses. As they played in the glistening gulf, the late-afternoon sun cast a golden trail across the surface of the water. It stretched, like a magic road, all the way to the horizon.

"Let's take a walk," Hal suggested.

"Let's get dressed," she responded.

"Ah, why spoil the fun? I like you like this!" He tweaked one of her nipples.

"That's why not!" Lisle exclaimed, and dashed off toward the car. "Nudity grabs your attention." She squeezed into an apple-green bikini, then turned with glee to watch Hal as he dressed.

"You grab my attention, woman, nude or not!" he admitted as he struggled into a brief swimsuit.

With both of them now properly, if skimpily, clad in bikinis, they started off down the sun-drenched beach, hand in hand.

"Now this has to be as beautiful as anything Cancun has to offer," he said.

"It's wonderful because you're here with me, Hal. You make my life so full. You're my compensation for all the unfairness I have to endure in my real world."

"Do you want to tell me what happened?"

She took a breath. "It's simple. I lost out to a younger woman. The boss decided to take five sleek young women to Cancun because they would be modeling bikinis."

"Instead of a lovely mature lady."

"No!" She exploded. "Forget age and maturity! I look as good as anybody in a bikini!"

Hal nodded. "Agreed!"

"But they didn't even consider that! They decided on age alone. Young. No one over forty. That eliminated me and Andrea right away. It's unfair, that's what! It just makes me so angry!"

"So, what can you do about it?"

"Nothing! Just do my best and try not to let things like this get under my skin."

"But they do."

"Damn right, they do! I do not like to be judged on my age alone! It's discriminatory and unfair!"

He offered a quiet resolution. "You could get out."

She halted disdainfully. "Get out? You mean, change companies? My agency is the only one that handles any model over fifty. There are no others for me to turn to."

"No. I mean quit."

"Quit? Quit working? And do what? Become your wife? To clean your two-story house? No, thanks!"

"God damn it, Lisle!"

"I'm sorry, Hal, I shouldn't have said that. I didn't mean it personally. I meant that generally housewifery isn't for me." They continued to walk.

"Lisle, I just don't understand you. Most women would jump at the chance I'm offering."

"I'm not most women!"

"Obviously! Well, what do you want? I love you as deeply as I possibly can, and I want to marry you. I want to stop this crazy business of meeting all over the country and settle down to living with you. And loving you."

"And to the dull routine of life?"

"Hell no!" He exploded, feeling suddenly as if he were being stretched out on a rack. "To . . . whatever life holds for us!"

"You mean, whatever *your* life holds."

"Lisle, I'm willing to marry you and make everything I own legally yours. You won't have to work again."

"My son, Craig," she said sarcastically, "would be eternally grateful to you for making an honest woman of his mother."

"You can share my life, my house, whatever I own. I want you to have everything I can give you. I want to take care of you, Lisle, so you won't have to lie in the goddamn snow to make a living or face any more discrimination because of your age—or anything else."

152

"You'll protect me? Tuck me away in some place safe from the big bad world?"

"Damn right! You would be respected as the classic beauty you are, and face no more battles for recognition."

"No more battles?"

"Life would be easy for you."

"In *your* world?"

"Yes, Lisle! Yes, damn it!"

Tears filled her eyes. "You still don't understand. You know me better than anyone else, Hal, including my own kids, and you still don't understand."

"Damnation! Understand? I understand that I've fallen in love with a complex lady. Just when I think I know what you want—love, security, marriage—you change."

"Oh, no, Hal. I haven't changed. That's what others want. Maybe what you want. But not me. You just didn't see the real me. You saw what you wanted to see. A woman who needed you."

"Well, don't you?"

Lisle looked at him long and hard. *"Need* you? No. I can take care of myself. But *want* you? Yes. However, on my terms, not yours."

He spread his hands. "What the hell are your terms? I've opened my heart—and now my guts—to you! It's your turn. Tell me what you want, Lisle?"

She said it simply, as if he should have known it all along. "I want independence. Independence for both of us. That's why I can't move into your home—your life. I have my own life. I've worked very hard to get it, for all its problems. And I want to keep it." She kicked at a shell.

Hal roared in frustration, "How the hell can both of us be independent in a marriage? You can do whatever you want to do, if that's what you mean."

She shook her head. "That's not what I mean. But I'm not sure exactly what I mean, and that's the catch! Hal, I've had the kind of life you're talking about, with my first husband.

153

We lived, quite nicely, in his world. We had a family, and we worked hard together. He took care of the finances; I took care of the home and kids. It worked out fine until he died. Only then did I realize that I looked to him for support, for happiness, for everything in my life. And he provided it sufficiently. However, I lost my own identity in the process. I was Mrs. Jack Wheaton. No one knew Lisle. Lisle? Who's that? Oh, Jack's wife."

"You've really taken this identity bit to heart, haven't you?" He looked at her curiously. Was this the same woman who met him eagerly at airports and laughed with him—and who had, only moments ago, lain nude in the sand making mad, passionate love?

"Oh, yes. I'm very serious. Thank God, I'm not Jack's widow anymore. Oh, I was for a while. I played that role to the hilt. Friends were sympathetic. I wallowed in my own inadequacies. What else could I do? I had no identity, other than being Jack's wife, and when he was gone, I became Jack's widow."

"When did you change?"

She sighed. "I met someone at a New Year's Eve party who made me realize how much I was depriving myself and my children."

"Was it a man? This Kaplan I keep hearing about?"

"No." Lisle laughed bitterly. "He came later, in my desperate search to regain my youth. No, this wasn't a man. Virginia was a widow, like myself, and I thought we'd have a lot in common. I couldn't have been further from the truth!"

"What did she tell you?"

"Are you sure you want to hear all this?"

"Oh, yes. I want to know anything that might help me understand you, Lisle, because I love you. And I fear we've reached an impasse."

"First, you have to realize what I was like, on that particular New Year's Eve." Lisle picked a spot and sat down on the sand. Hal joined her.

154

"Life without Jack was very difficult for me—and the kids —and I had taken on the impossible burden of being mother, father, friend—everything—to them. I was pretty miserable company, and God knows why my friends invited me to the party, except that they probably felt sorry for me. I agreed to come because I figured the hostess and I could wallow in our misery together, since we were both widows. Well, she was far too busy to wallow with me!

"I sat in a corner, with my little glass of champagne, and watched the most attractive and dynamic woman I'd ever met! She was president of her own company, a stockholder in another, and had just finished taking flying lessons! She was living every day to the fullest, though she must have been at least sixty! The next day, New Year's Day, mind you, I called and invited her to lunch. That, for me, was a bold act. And the beginning."

He smiled wryly. "The new Lisle."

She nodded. "The beginning of a new year is often a time for reflection and looking back to see how far you've come, and I hadn't come very far in the years since Jack's death. New Year's Day is also a time of looking ahead. Obviously, my future looked empty."

"I can't imagine you like that, Lisle."

"Well," she said, chuckling ruefully, "I told you I was pretty miserable. Virginia and I became fast friends. She taught me to accept myself and determine what I had to offer myself and my kids. It took me a while to figure it out because I had always been Jack's helpmate. My change was gradual. Actually, it's an ongoing thing, Hal. I'm still changing and hope I always will. But it's a good feeling because when I look ahead, I know the best is yet to come."

"I'd like to think the best is yet to come for *us* too, Lisle."

Abruptly she stood and began walking down the empty beach again. He followed, staying just close enough to hear her. "Don't you see, Hal? I'm afraid I'll go back to my old life if I marry you. Only this time I'll be Mrs. Hal Kammerman—Hal's wife." She shook her head vehemently. "I can't do it. I've come too far."

They walked again, in silence. Finally Hal spoke, "So, this is it? Our relationship has to exist in a fantasy world, if at all?"

"You must admit, Hal, it's been fun." She turned and laid her hand on his arm. "It's been wonderful."

"But what you're telling me is that it can't grow." He shifted, wanting to escape her touch and feeling an emptiness inside as real as the emptiness of the beach where they walked.

"Yes, it can." But she doubted her own words. She honestly didn't know how it could grow.

Hal walked on ahead without her, wandering into the softly lapping waves of the gulf, then back to more solid sand. Lisle followed, adding her footprints to his in the sand. They left a meandering trail of intermingling footprints along the beach.

"Hal, wait for me," she called, hurrying to catch up.

He halted and looked out across the expanse of glistening water. "Why should I wait any longer? It's useless," he said. "I feel that this is the end for us, Lisle."

She stopped suddenly, chilled by his words. "It doesn't have to be."

"That's what you seem to be telling me."

"Why can't we stay the same? Hal, I just want to stand on my own two feet, not lean on you."

He wheeled around, his blue eyes piercing into her. "Is it possible, Lisle?"

"I hope so," she said dispiritedly.

Behind her was the trail of their footprints in the sand. He could see two distinct and separate trails. Together, but separate. Was the best yet to come for them? Hal couldn't imagine it.

What the hell was wrong with him? Here he was making every effort to change in Lisle exactly what he loved about her! She was unique and complex and damned independent. She had a vitality that he loved and needed. And now he wanted to turn her into his wife—Hal's wife. "I just want to know one thing, Lisle."

She blinked and nodded silently.

They stood a good twenty feet apart, so his words were loud. "Do you love me?"

Without hesitation she answered "Yes." She had never before said it, not even to herself, but she had known all along. . . . "I could never have stayed with you in New Hampshire if I didn't love you, Hal."

"Well, then—" He halted and looked at her expectantly.

"Well, then—what?" Lisle demanded, hands on her hips in frustration. What more did he want from her? She had just spilled her guts and in doing so had maybe even ruined their relationship.

"Well, then"—he heaved a long sigh—"I only know it gets damned lonely out there in the real world."

"Oh, Hal—" She sprinted into his arms. He was warm and secure and could love her better than anyone else in the world. He was her hero; her Viking with gentle blue eyes and a tough spirit; her pirate, strong but tender.

Yet could Hal keep her from being lonely out there in the world and offer her the independence she needed? Could they walk separate paths but remain together? Could they grow as individuals, or would that growth pull them apart? If they continued living and working apart, would the fabric of their relationship be strong enough to hold them together? Or was it inevitable that they would part?

When they left Florida at the end of the week, there were still no answers.

CHAPTER TEN

It seemed a perfectly natural thing for her to do, and Lisle picked up the phone to dial Hal's number. That she did so with noticeable ease was indeed remarkable, given all her earlier resistance to anything that would bring together their very separate lives. She smiled, happily anticipating his answer, and wondered why she hadn't asked him to do this long before now. It was logical, long overdue, and a damn good idea!

"Hello?"

As always, upon hearing his rumbling, masculine voice, she felt a heart-pounding expectancy. "Hal? This is—"

"Lisle! How are you? It's good to hear your voice tonight. I was just thinking of you."

"That's a great opening line, and true or not, I love to hear it."

"I swear it's true. How has your week been?"

"It was okay. Odessa was windy and cold, but the turnout was better than I expected. We were the biggest show in town. That should give you some idea of the size of the place."

"Are you all right, Lisle?" He sensed she was calling for some reason other than to chat about the weather in Odessa.

"I'm fine. I just called to see if you can get away a few hours earlier next week. And fly here to Dallas." She hesitated, waiting for a reaction to the invitation.

He paused too. "Instead of our trip to Cancun?" *Canceled again* was his first thought.

"Oh, no," she hurried to explain. "We would still go down to Cancun as planned. My children want to meet you, Hal, and I think it's a good idea. I have a spring show that day, at the Anatole Hotel, near the courtyard. It would be a nice time for you to meet them."

"Oh? Finally taking me home to meet the family, huh?"

"I hope you don't mind being grilled about your job, stability, and possibly your ancestry. My kids are particular about whom their mother brings home."

"Well, don't you think it's about time they took notice of your activities? I've been saying that all along."

"So have they," she drawled. "My children are curious about this man I've been seeing for months, and frankly, they're quite anxious to meet you. If it's okay with you, you could come early and attend the Spring Gala Fashion Show, starring yours truly. Afterwards we could all meet for a late lunch, have a pleasant little chitchat with my kids, then be on our way. We could both take the same flight to Cancun— the one I'm already scheduled to take. Then we'd be alone for a week. How does that sound?"

"Sounds as though you have it all planned. Is it what you want, Lisle? Do you really want me there, or are you doing this because of pressure from your kids?"

"Both," she admitted, then added earnestly, "I want you here, Hal. It's been lonely without you."

"Then I'll be there."

The day of the show was hectic, as usual. By the time Hal's cab arrived, Lisle was already a nervous wreck. She told herself it was not because Hal would soon be meeting her children. What difference did it really make if they liked one another? She cared for Hal and wouldn't stop seeing him merely because of their approval or disapproval. Their loud objections hadn't stopped her yet.

159

Still, horrible thoughts overshadowed her every move as she tried to apply mascara without brushing her cheek and eyelid. Lisle had never been so nervous about a show, especially one on her home turf. At the exclusive Anatole Hotel they could expect only the most gracious of receptions. But Hal had never watched her in a show. What if she stumbled? She stood back from the mirror to appraise her subtle eye makeup. She was being silly. She was, after all, a professional. Professionals didn't stumble. *But sometimes real people fell on their faces!*

What if Craig created a scene, demanding that they either make a decision to marry or end this foolishness? Oh, Hal would probably be very happy about that! Oh, God, she prayed. *Don't let anything awful happen!*

Realistically, Lisle knew Hal would make a good impression on her family. He was a gentleman and could talk to anyone. He would be able to talk politics or business with Craig. She was certain that somehow he would be able to soothe Craig's irritation over their affair without having to confront the big decision. Whether to love or leave.

"Lisle?"

Wheeling around, Lisle encountered Hal's handsome face. "What are you doing in here?" She pushed him out of the tiny dressing area she shared with five other models. "Hal! There are other women dressing in here, you know!"

He grinned rakishly. "Perhaps I could help zip them up." Warm masculine hands cupped her face gently. "But rest assured, Lisle, I only have eyes for you." He kissed her, his hands and lips warming the quivering emotions behind her cool facade. Why couldn't they escape right now? Oh, how she wished they could fly away together and avoid the fashion show and the showdown with her kids!

"Hal," she said softly, then kissed him ardently. She would have to repair her makeup, but she didn't care. Touching him gave her strength and confidence, both of which she needed right now.

"I'll be watching for you, Lisle. You're beautiful, you know. And don't worry about that meeting with your kids. I'll be on my best behavior."

"I'm not worried, Hal," she protested, albeit weakly.

His thumbs wiped at the crease along her brow. "Uh-huh. I know. I promise to keep the club and loincloth hidden until we get to Cancun. But after we arrive, I warn you, I'll chase you down the beach!" He paused as one of the models slithered past them, then added, "In the nude!"

"Hal!" She laughed, amused as she pictured the two of them running down a beach in the buff.

He kissed her again, quickly, and was gone, leaving her smiling and encouraged. She was sure that was his intent. He knew her so well, realized she'd be nervous, remembered what would make her laugh. Her wild fantasies! A club and a loincloth, indeed! Lisle had to admit, she was lucky to have a man like Hal Kammerman who cared for her and wanted to make her laugh. And, if she believed him, loved her.

A demanding male voice jolted her back to the work ahead. "Less than ten minutes, ladies! How are we doing in here? Everybody got everything they need?"

Lisle turned back to the mirror and began a hurried repair of her makeup.

The show was about to begin when Hal heard his name.

"Hal? Hal Kammerman? Is it—" The woman paused as Hal turned to see who it was who knew his name. "Is it possible? Is it really you, way out here in Texas?"

Hal gaped at the copper-haired beauty. Her hair had a slightly windblown look, and her huge chestnut eyes were gentle and contented. She was ravishing in a red silk dress that curved around her full bosom and hugged her shapely hips.

She smiled hesitantly. "Well—don't you recognize me?"

When he finally found his voice, Hal rasped, "Kathryn! Kathryn Coleman!"

161

Immediately their bodies melded together in a long-held embrace—the embrace of old friends who haven't seen each other in years. Finally he held her at arm's length and murmured, "Kathryn, Kathryn," as if trying to convince himself it was really she.

"I haven't heard that name in years, Hal," she admonished gently. "I'm Kaye Logan now. New life-style, family, and name."

"It has been years, hasn't it? God! You look great! What a coincidence to run into you here!"

She laughed in that easy, natural way of hers and said, "Well, I'm here to represent the Leukemia Society, which is one of the charities benefiting from the style show today. It's customary for me to make an appearance. But you are the one out of pocket. What in the world are you doing here, Hal? It's a long way from Delaware."

"I'm here to see my fri—" He started to say "friend," but quickly changed it to "fiancée." Not exactly true, but it was the closest he could come to saying, "We're lovers." "Lisle's modeling in the show today."

"Your fiancée is a model? How interesting. Did you say her name is Lisle?"

He nodded. "Lisle Wheaton. Do you know her?" Was it possible? He held his breath.

"Lisle Wheaton? Her name is definitely familiar. I think I've read about her."

"You'll probably recognize her when you see her," he replied. "She's frequently in national magazines. If I sound proud, it's because I am. She's very special to me."

Kaye took his hand in both of hers. "I'm glad, Hal. Really glad. You deserve all the happiness in the world. Now, let's have a seat and you can tell me all about her. And you."

Kaye pulled him to a corner table near the courtyard so they could chat. When Lisle started to glide down the runway, Hal gestured proudly. "There she is." Lisle pivoted in front of them, and he beamed with pride.

"You're right, Hal. She's absolutely lovely." Kaye smiled approvingly. "And I do recognize her face. I've seen her on a magazine cover, just recently. Is she from Texas?"

He nodded. "There's something about those beautiful Texas women," Hal admitted with a glimmer in his eyes, "that I can't resist."

"They say it's the humidity." Kaye shrugged, patting a flawless cheek.

"Whatever it is, it's certainly good for you, Kaye. You look absolutely radiant!" His hands covered hers affectionately and brought them to his lips. He kissed their well-manicured tips, relishing their smoothness. "Some things never change. Your hands are still beautiful. And so are you."

"But some things do change, drastically!" Kaye laughed delightedly and shared a secret. "I hate to disappoint you, but this glow is from hormones, not humidity. I'm pregnant, Hal."

"P-pregnant?" He stammered the word. "How wonderful! You must be thrilled!" A new admiration filled his eyes.

Kaye's manner was almost offhand. "This will be number two for us. We already have Matthew junior, who's two and a half. He's a regular little hellion! Takes after his father's side of the family!" She laughed at her own joke, as only a loving wife would.

"It's obvious that you're happy, Kaye."

"Oh, yes." She beamed. "Matt's a state senator now, you know. We have a good life together." They were so absorbed in each other, they missed Lisle's subsequent appearances in the show. It did not go unnoticed.

Hal nodded. "I see your husband's name in the papers occasionally. He's a damn lucky man! What about your antique business? Now that you're married to an active politician and busy having children, have you shelved that project?"

"Oh, heavens no! We have two shops here in Dallas, another one in Fort Worth, and plans for a Houston branch in the future. We hired managers for each store, and I oversee their functions and do the buying. I try to schedule my buying trips in conjunction with some of Matt's travel. Remember that first auction you and I attended years ago, Hal?"

"Oh, yes. Two greenhorns!" He laughed and rolled his eyes.

"Well, I've learned a lot about auctions since then. I'll bet I've attended a hundred, and they're still exciting to me."

"What about your family? How do you manage all this traveling and going to auctions and overseeing stores?"

She smiled brightly. "Just like any other working wife and mother. I have help. It's a whole new world for me, Hal. I'll admit that sometimes it gets pretty hectic around our house, but I love it." The smile on her face mirrored her inner happiness.

"It's a relief to see you so obviously happy, Kaye. I spent many a day—and night—worrying about you." He squeezed her hands lovingly, making no effort to hide his affection.

"I know. And I appreciate it. It was nice to know there was someone around who cared for me when things were going rough. I'll never forget all you did for me, Hal, especially your caring. I always knew I could rely on you. Now"—she smiled gaily—"tell me all about you and Lisle. How did you meet her?"

He took a deep breath. "It's a long story. . . ."

Hal and Kaye were so busy catching up on the last few years of their lives that they hardly noticed the rest of the style show, or Lisle.

She figured she could have stumbled and fallen clean off the elevated runway, and they wouldn't have seen her. Hal only had eyes for the young woman at his table. And she was much younger than Lisle. When the show was over, Lisle took her time removing her eye makeup and changing to her own classy traveling clothes. She was the last to leave the tiny dressing room.

Walking slowly, she could see Hal sitting alone at the courtyard table. Thank God, the attractive copper-haired woman in the red dress was gone.

Hal rose and kissed her cheek. "You were great, Lisle! Prettiest one in the show."

She smiled weakly. How would he know? He scarcely saw the show! "Are you ready to be grilled by my children?" Lisle led the way across the open courtyard to the restaurant where they had planned to meet Inga and Craig. She spotted Craig, already waiting for them.

As expected, Hal was charming with her children, but she watched their interaction with detached interest. What had previously seemed crucial didn't matter anymore. Losing out to younger women was becoming a pattern in her life.

Hal and Craig—they seemed cut from the same cloth— discussed politics and economic trends. Lisle feared they would blow it all by tackling religion next. But they didn't. And much to her relief, her brash young son didn't face Hal with "Now, sir, just what are your intentions with respect to my mother?" Actually, they didn't discuss Lisle at all.

When Inga arrived, late and slightly bedraggled, Hal turned his full attention to her. Before long they were discussing the hassles of dealing with small children and her first IRS forms as a single parent.

As lunch drew to a close Craig discreetly gave Lisle the okay sign with his thumb and forefinger. Lisle smiled appreciatively at her son. Hal had won the approval of his toughest critic.

Before leaving the restaurant, Lisle and Inga slipped into the ladies' room.

"Mother! He's fascinating! And so handsome! I love the gray in his hair. It's very distinguished-looking."

Lisle brushed her hair with long strokes. "I told you he was handsome."

"I can understand why you're so attracted to him. He seems just right for you. Intelligent, handsome—"

165

"My age!" Lisle finished.

"Now, Mother. I wasn't going to mention that."

Lisle sighed heavily and lifted apologetic eyes to her daughter. "Sorry, Inga. I shouldn't have brought it up." She turned to go, but Inga's hand caught her arm.

"Mother, I think Hal loves you. You can see it in his eyes."

Lisle looked solemnly at her daughter. "So he claims," she said as doubts raced through her mind.

Hal slammed his suitcase into the corner of their suite at El Presidente, one of Cancun's finest hotels. "Okay, Lisle. What the hell is wrong with you?"

"Nothing!" She plunked her suitcase on the other side of the bed and began rummaging through it.

"Nothing?" He spoke mockingly. " 'Nothing' made you tight as a clam at lunch with your own kids? 'Nothing' made you uncharacteristically quiet on the entire three-hour flight from Dallas to Cancun? What happened to the lady who enjoyed taking flights of fancy with her lover?"

"Please, Hal. I'm tired." She began to remove her traveling suit to change to casual slacks and a pullover.

"And I suppose you have a headache too. Tell me what's wrong," he demanded. "Didn't I pass muster with your children? Well, I can tell you right now—"

She held up a hand to hush him. "Both of them think you're marvelous, Hal. You passed with flying colors. They seem to think you're perfect for me."

"Do you?"

"At the present time? I don't know!" She pulled on the lightweight jersey.

"Aha! We're narrowing the problem through this stupid little game of charades. So the problem lies with you, not your kids!"

"The problem lies," she snapped, "with you! I'm getting tired of losing out to younger women!"

166

"What the hell do you mean by that?" He grasped her arms with uncharacteristic force.

Lisle clenched her teeth and muttered, "Who is she, Hal? The younger woman in the red silk dress!"

CHAPTER ELEVEN

Hal's hard grip on her arms didn't lessen. "Who is *she?* What woman are you talking about, Lisle?"

"I'm referring to the woman you were with today during the style show. My show!" It was humiliating to have to say it—it was of course an accusation of infidelity. But by his damnable pretense of ignorance Hal had forced her to do it. She just had to ask about the other woman. She couldn't stop herself and yet hated herself—and him—now that she had spoken the demeaning words.

What allegiance, if any, did Hal owe her? *That* was the heart of the matter! Meeting in different parts of the country for the occasional liaison would not build a loyal and faithful bond between them. One day the flimsy thread that held them together would break, and Hal would be gone from her life. She would not have the strength to repair their relationship—their love. Lisle choked with emotion, feeling rage, jealousy, fear.

He stared at her in disbelief. "The woman—"

Lisle, nearly hysterical, rambled incoherently: "The woman you embraced so lovingly and hovered over—holding hands openly during my show. Right under my nose! How dare you flaunt another woman in my presence!"

"Lisle . . . Lisle, my God." He chuckled soothingly. "There's no need to be so upset. This little fit of jealousy doesn't become you. I can't believe you're behaving this

168

way." He eased his viselike grip and slid his hands down her arms, stopping to caress her wrists.

"A little fit of jealousy?" she spat out. "How can you be so damned blasé? When the same thing happened with Kaplan, I swore I wouldn't be duped ever again! But I've been taken in by your charms. I loved you, Hal Kammerman, and thought I could trust you! But here it is happening again!" Lisle was shaking all over and could feel the hot sting of tears.

He narrowed his eyes angrily. "Lisle, you aren't making much sense. I don't know what in hell you're talking about, but I'd certainly like to know. The woman you're apparently so hot over is Kathryn Coleman Logan, an old family friend."

"Old? Ha! An old family friend?" She gasped. "That's an old excuse!"

"Excuse? My God, Lisle! Kaye's the wife of a Texas senator!"

"That's even worse! You're coming on to a young, attractive woman who's married to a politician, yet! Hal, are you crazy?" She jerked away from his hands.

"Since you're so intent on finding me guilty before my trial, add this to your list of circumstantial evidence, Lisle," Hal barked, maliciously fueling her fire. "She's pregnant too! And she already has one child! We tried to keep it hidden but just couldn't contain ourselves any longer!"

"Hal, don't be such a jackass!" Lisle spoke in a near wail. "If you two have nothing to hide, and she really is an old friend, why didn't she wait around to meet me?"

He shrugged. "Hell, I don't know. You took forever, and she said she had to meet her husband at some political function."

"All right, all right! Forget it, Hal! Please get out of my way. I need some fresh air and room to think. I don't care about you or her or your old excuses!" Lisle pushed past him and grabbed the doorknob. The door would not open, which took some of the punch out of her exit. She rattled it, shook it, struggled fruitlessly to get it open.

"Where do you think you're going?" He stood behind her, his fists on his hips.

"I—I have to get out of here before the walls close in on me. I need to walk and think and clear my mind. This has been a nerve-racking day for me. The kids, the job, you. And now this other-woman business! I'm not sure I'm even thinking straight." She pulled frantically on the stubborn door, finally sputtering, "Damned Mexican doors! Open it for me, please."

Hal reached over her fumbling fingers and gripped the knob firmly. One hard jerk and the door was open. "I'm going with you, Lisle," he declared with finality.

"Didn't you get the message? I don't want you to go with me."

"There will be no walking alone in a strange place," Hal replied firmly, and followed her. "Especially a foreign country."

Lisle ignored him, or tried to, as she marched off through the open courtyard of the elegant hotel. The abundant tropical foliage perfumed the air, and the atmosphere was altogether musical and beautiful. This was definitely a place for lovers, and Lisle wished that she hadn't come. Unfortunately, her dramatic exit had been foiled when the blasted door stuck. Then she even had to stop and ask Hal to open it for her! Damn! She couldn't even be mad properly.

Mustering her haughty reserve, Lisle tried to regain her composure as she walked past the outdoor restaurants and a mariachi band blasting festive music to happy tourists. Oh, God, she couldn't wait to get away from them!

She stumbled down rock steps, past several shimmering pools and another thatch-roofed bar, and across a large stretch of sand. Hal followed closely behind. She found it damned hard to walk with dignity, as she felt herself moving

170

along in slow motion, sinking deeper in the sand with each step.

Finally Lisle reached the hard-packed beach. Her refuge. Somehow this place where land met the ocean restored her sense of stability. She took a deep breath, inhaling the warm, salty air. The hotel was located on the bay side of the inlet, and the gentle waves lapped softly at the sand.

Lisle walked along the edge of the white sands, letting the waves wash over her feet. The water felt cool and fresh, and she bent to touch it with trembling fingers.

What the hell was wrong with her? Today she had amplified a misunderstanding with Hal, had in fact seriously over-reacted! All along, Lisle had told herself that she and Hal could easily end their affair—there would be no unbreakable bonds. She professed not to want or need his love, nor did she want to be bound to him.

But her erratic actions today defeated her proclaimed resistance. Suddenly, when Hal was so obviously entranced by another woman, she acted like any jealous female trying to regain her man. And God knows, she had stubbornly resisted that possessiveness all along. Lisle wanted to be free and independent. And she wanted the same for Hal.

Given those terms, however, what would hold them together? Would they continue these crazy flights of fancy until someone else who loved and needed him fell into his arms? Tears of sad frustration rolled down her face. Lisle could feel Hal's presence, but he didn't say a thing. He just waited for her to calm down. Waited for her to speak. Why the hell did he hang around? Why didn't he just leave her? She didn't deserve his devotion!

Lisle stood and spoke in a low, apologetic tone. "I guess you think I'm pretty hotheaded. I feel like a jealous fool. I'm sorry, Hal. I don't know what got into me today."

He placed his arm loosely around her shoulders. "Lisle, we decided to fly down here to Cancun to recapture some intangible thing we thought was missing when you lost that

171

location assignment. Somehow, coming here in spite of everything would prove that our relationship, even perhaps our love, was strong, regardless of outside influences such as job, family . . . even other women."

She sighed shakily, eyes still brimming with tears. "You're right, Hal. And I almost blew it. Maybe I did blow it with my little jealous fit. I just couldn't stand the thought of you with someone else."

"No, you didn't blow it. But it shows that we definitely need to communicate better. About everything. Our past. Our feelings. Even our fears. At the risk of losing what is most important to me, I'd like to tell you about that other woman you saw me with today."

Lisle looked up at him, surprise and dread in her eyes. Oh, God—she did not want to hear this. "You don't have to, Hal. I . . . believe you when you say she's an old friend."

"I want to tell you about her. You should know what place she had in my life." Hal began. "Kay Logan was married to a man who was a very good friend of mine in Delaware. She was Kathryn Coleman then, and she and Emery spent a great deal of time with Beth and me. She was quite young, very pretty, and Emery treated her like a queen. The four of us partied on weekends, went sailing on Sundays, generally had a lot of fun together. Even after Beth died, the three of us remained close friends.

"When Emery died suddenly, he left massive debts. By the time Kathryn, er, Kaye paid them all off, she was nearly destitute, with only a single piece of property in Texas that wouldn't sell. Because I had been Emery's friend and confidant, I felt particularly responsible for his wife and tried to persuade her not to go to Texas. I guess my intention was to take over where Emery had left off and continue treating her like a queen. And I wanted her . . . near me."

"Did you love her?"

His voice grew ragged. "I thought I did. I even offered her marriage as financial security."

172

"But she refused?"

He nodded. "I was wrong. What I thought was abiding love was more of a brotherly love, maybe even fatherly. I hated to see Kathryn so unhappy and wanted to protect her. I even offered her sanctuary in my home in Delaware. But she would have none of it."

"Is that what you're offering me, Hal. Sanctuary?"

"No. I don't want a sexless marriage with you, Lisle. You see, Kathryn and I were never lovers. A marriage with her would have been in name only. I—I couldn't bear that with you. I love you too much and want to show it in all ways, including physically."

"Hal, you don't have to tell me this."

"It's the truth. I didn't really love her, Lisle. It was nothing like what you and I share. I love you with a deeper devotion than I ever dreamed possible with any woman. Any woman, including Beth. Look at me." He lifted her chin. "Do you believe me?"

She nodded, unable to respond. She wanted to believe him. Lisle's heart wrenched as she wrung out the words: "Kaye was someone you would have married, if circumstances had been right. You could have loved her. She could have learned to love you."

"No, God damn it!" he burst forth. "I couldn't have loved her. Ever! We wouldn't have had a marriage. I would have been more a guardian than a husband to her. I swear I love you, Lisle! Only you! Now, why can't you believe me?"

"I do, Hal. It's just my damned crazy imagination. You two seemed so attuned to each other today. You only had eyes for her. And she was giving you her undivided attention."

"I'm sorry about that, Lisle. But we hadn't seen each other since she married this football-playing Texan, and now she has a little son and is expecting again. We had so much to talk about."

"Well, you certainly did that." She sniffed indignantly.

173

"Lisle, do you trust me?"

She nodded again but avoided his eyes.

"Then why do you continue to doubt me? That isn't like you, Lisle. Why?"

Lisle sighed shakily. Hal's words dug into her, and she lifted her head. "Yes, Hal. You deserve to know why I acted like such an idiot today. I—I'm embarrassed. Throwing such a fit over someone who proved to be an old family friend is . . . childish, but I couldn't control myself."

"Then talk to me about it. That's the only way we can grow, Lisle. The only way we can maintain our relationship is to share these things, no matter how much they hurt."

"You're right, of course," she agreed, wringing her hands. "Oh, hell. I might as well just tell you. Then you'll understand. You know about my affair with Kaplan. He was young and handsome, and I was flattered that I could attract a man ten years younger than myself. We had fun together, and naively I trusted him implicitly. One evening we attended a party given by one of the models at work. She was young and beautiful, and Kaplan found her enchanting. That night I took a cab home. I lost out to a younger woman.

"It was very embarrassing. The word spread like wildfire at work and to the local press. They found us an interesting item because Craig was running for office at the time and I'm a kind of celebrity back home. You know how they like to exaggerate everything in an election year. Then they found out about the *Playboy* article! So when I went to Grand Manan, I just wanted to escape completely.

"Can you see why I wanted to keep our love a fantasy? To keep you away from all this? And to protect myself. When I saw you today with that beautiful young woman, I thought I was losing again. And I couldn't stand the thought, Hal. Because I love you."

He wrapped his comforting arms around her. "Lisle, you must know by now that I love only you. I can forget Kaplan

174

and what he did to your life if you can forget Kathryn's place in mine. They aren't a part of our lives anymore. The past doesn't matter. Our love is for the present, and the future." He pulled her close, and she fell willingly into his arms.

"Hold me, Hal. Just hold me. I do love you," Lisle murmured. In his arms Lisle could soar to the sky, could defeat any foe, even escape to a fantasy island with her hero. She breathed in his impeccably masculine scent and was gripped by an overwhelming desire to run her hand over his skin and kiss his chest. She wanted to press him into her with all her might.

Lisle clung to him, light-headed with relief. This had been a day full of anxieties and pressures. Now, though, in Hal's arms all of that could be forgotten. He would keep her secure and stable. He loved her. She could feel it. She raised her face longingly to meet his kiss. Was this what it was all about? She knew that when Hal was with her, she could accomplish any feat. Conquer anything. And just bringing her lips into contact with his made her yearn to lie with him, feel the warmth of his bare skin, and take whatever he could offer.

"Hal, I hope I haven't ruined our whole week. This trip was to be special for us."

"It will be special, Lisle. It's times like this that bring us closer than ever. Both of us have revealed parts of our past that still hurt and affect us today. That's important for us to know. It'll make our relationship stronger."

"Stronger, Hal? It almost ruined it for us. _I_ almost ruined it."

"No, my dear. Nothing could ruin it. I love you too much, Lisle."

"I don't want to lose what we have," she whispered.

He kissed her again, his lips taking ardent possession of hers. He pressed her length to him and whispered against her ear, "I want you, Lisle. Can you feel my desire?"

"Oh, yes." She laughed. "I think you're horny!"

"It's been four weeks, two days, and fourteen long hours since we last made love, and I have been with you practically all day, watching you, but not touching. That's asking too much! I'm going crazy! Anyway," he murmured gruffly as his lips sought her earlobe, "I promised you a romp on the beach, in the buff! Then I want to ravage your sweet body. Why not now?"

"Hal, there are too many people around here."

"I'll bet we could find a secluded spot, like we did in Florida."

His kiss halted any further response, and Lisle allowed herself to relax in his arms. She felt the warmth of desire spreading through her limbs and knew that she, too, wanted to find a secluded spot on the beach. Then a horrible thought struck her.

"No, Hal! There might be hermit crabs! Or night crawlers on the sand!"

"You didn't say that in Florida!"

"It was daylight. We could see!"

"But who was looking for hermit crabs?" He laughed. "I'll race you back to the room!" Hand in hand, they ran back to the hotel, past the cabana and pools and happy mariachis. They were a different couple this time, passionate for each other, intent on being alone.

The door was their only obstacle, and it wasn't about to give freely now. No matter how much fumbling, struggling, or kicking was applied, the door held. Lisle leaned breathless against the wall and laughed while Hal struggled feverishly to open the door.

"Damned Mexican doors!" He applied one shoulder to the door, then—with anger fueling the force of his movements—gave it a final push and burst into the room.

Rolling with laughter, they fell into each other's arms on the bed.

"I'll speak to the manager tomorrow," he promised. "We

can't go through a test of strength every time we want to leave or enter the room. This is supposed to be a swanky place."

"Shhhh," she whispered. "We may never want to leave. At least no one will break into our room!"

"They would only find"—he pulled her jersey over her head and kissed her delicate breasts—"two people in love and making mad, passionate love."

His lips tugged fervently on the rosy tips until they were firm, aching morsels in his mouth. His hands encased her ribs and slid down to her hips, removing her slacks in the process. After a brief pause to remove his own clothes, he was beside her, nude. He kissed her and loved, caressed, and touched her everywhere. Her body was alive with the fire of passion held repressed for weeks, and she responded eagerly to his every stroke.

He moved down her waist, across the firm white expanse of her stomach. "How can I convince you that I love only you? I want your body next to mine, Lisle, sharing the pleasures we can give each other."

"Yes, yes. I believe you, Hal. I do trust you. I—I don't want to lose you." She knew, at that moment, she would do anything to keep Hal. He was too important to her—she couldn't risk losing him.

His lips were burning tiny trails of fire along her inner thighs, all the way to the center of her sensitivity. "Only if we were married . . ." His tongue sought that sensitive bud, and she gasped audibly.

"What . . . Oh—" She moaned softly as her flesh blazed under his manipulations.

"If we were married, my love, you would be assured of my unfailing love and devotion to you. And yours to me." He continued his maddening stimulation.

Hal kissed her tender, aching skin, until Lisle begged for his fulfillment. He shifted his muscular frame between the vise of her legs, molding himself to her entire length. She could feel him—masculine, hard, aroused.

"Yes! Yes! Don't wait any longer, Hal!" She dug her fingers into his buttocks.

"Now, Lisle? Tell me you need my love!"

"Yes," she whispered, then cried out in joy as he plunged into her. "I need you, Hal."

"Then marry me, Lisle! I need you too." He said it as he moved with her rhythm.

"Yes! Yes, Hal." Lisle could hardly think straight as she reached new heights of ecstasy.

Her name and words of love and desire fell from his lips as they rode to the highest crest of love's peak. Lisle had never felt the full surge of Hal's power as she did tonight. Perhaps her love and longing for him made it all stronger, more meaningful. As they settled slowly, floatingly, down from the summit, Lisle felt the sting of tears.

"Lisle, what's wrong?"

She buried her face in his heaving chest. "It's just that I know I love you so much, Hal."

He cuddled her to him, and after a while he said, "Lisle, we have to talk about what happens next."

"What do you mean?"

"It's up to you, Lisle. The decision is yours. If it's yes, we'll have love ever after. If it's no, I'll be out on the street."

"What? Why?"

"Because I finally sold the house."

"Ohhh, Hal." She groaned. "Your house—"

"Lisle, I love you. Marry me. I need you, and I hope you need me." Their desire became an expression of loving concern and understanding. He held her and loved her all night long, lavishing her with gentle words and caresses, and Lisle knew she would never be lonely again.

Gingerly, using the pads of her fingers, Lisle stretched nude panty hose along a shapely, extended leg. Sliding the other leg in, she stood and pulled the hose over her slender hips. "Hal, this is crazy. Absolutely wild!" In the light of day she was definitely having second thoughts.

"No, it isn't! No crazier than anything else we've done! This goes right along with pirates and Vikings." He wasn't giving her a chance to think twice, or to back out. "Just imagine, Lisle, what a romantic resolution for the ruthless Viking and his fair captive!"

"Somehow, this isn't how I pictured it." Lisle slipped a burgundy silk dress over her head and scrutinized her image in the mirror. "This isn't why we came to Mexico, Hal. We came to recapture the fantasy, not destroy it. I don't think I'm dressed appropriately. I intended to wear this dress in the evening, for dining and dancing."

"We can do that too." He helped her fasten the tiny buttons at the back of her dress. "You're beautiful, my love."

"Crazy, that's what it is!"

Hal reached for the door. "Ready? You've never looked lovelier." They hadn't gotten around to complaining about the door, so leaving took a few minutes of struggling. After a few choice expletives he managed to wrest the door open. "Damned Mexican doors," he muttered as they hurried out to the waiting cab. "I've got to see that manager."

"Don't bother." She grinned. "It's part of the ambience here." She climbed into the cab, ignoring Hal's continued grumbling. As he gave the address to the driver, she focused on the lively decorations around the front windshield. A fringe draped the entire length of the window and framed a reassuring sign in elaborately lettered Spanish. Roughly translated, it read *God Goes with This Car.*

Suddenly they swung out into the traffic, and Lisle's eyes tried to catch the sign again and pray at the same time! All she could see was that fringe and its tiny balls bobbing violently. They switched lanes three times in the course of a block, and Lisle latched on to Hal's leg with a determined grip.

"Hal! Did you see that—Oh, my God! We're going to be killed in a foreign country!"

He patted her hand. "Take it easy, my love. This is just part of the ambience down here. They all drive this way."

The driver wheeled around a corner, tires whining, and, with a burst of speed, managed to glide neatly in front of a bus. The blare of a horn blocked out Lisle's hastily muttered prayer.

She clapped her hands over her eyes. "I can't watch this massacre! Not when it's going to be us!"

Hal leaned forward. "Eh, *señor*. Slow down, *por favor*. You're scaring the lady."

The driver smiled broadly, white teeth gleaming beneath his dark, bushy mustache. *"Sí, señor."*

If anything, he increased the speed, for they whizzed past charming buildings and down narrow winding streets. Not once were they held up by a traffic light. With a dramatic screech of the tires the cab finally halted in front of a faded pink adobe church. Lisle scrambled out, barely resisting the urge to flatten herself on the dusty earth and give it a re- sounding kiss. Hal gave the driver a handful of pesos and uttered a hearty *"Adiós!* We'll walk back!"

Lisle looked up at the church, then back to Hal. "A prayer of thanksgiving seems appropriate about now."

He chuckled. "Hell of a ride, wasn't it? Are you okay?"

"I'm a little weak-kneed. But I don't know if it's the wild ride or the crazy thing we're about to do."

"Do you want to back out?"

She took a deep breath. Were they doing the right thing? Oh, God—this was no time to be asking. She should be sure. Then why wasn't she? "Hal, what do I say again?" she asked hesitantly.

"Te acepto a ti. Sí, mi amor. You just say *sí* to everything." He laughed and kissed her forehead. His hand pressed at her back, steering her into the dark interior of the tiny church, past heavy religious carvings to the flower-bedecked altar.

180

Suddenly serious, they stood humbly before the dark-skinned black-robed priest. He smiled and greeted them . . . in Spanish. Thoughts whirled through Lisle's head. *This is like a dream! Say yes to everything. Sí, sí . . .*

The priest read the phrases in rapid Spanish: *"Habeis venido aquí, hermanos, para que el Señor, ante el ministro de la Iglesia y ante esta unidad Christiana, consagre con su sello vuestro amor. Este amor Cristo . . ."*

CHAPTER TWELVE

The golden beaches and the lace-edged surf of Cancun receded as the jet soared above the earth. This exotic fantasy of a place, so warm and beautiful, had a magical, almost dreamlike quality. And the events that had taken place in Lisle's life during the last five days were themselves the stuff of magic and dreams. She was a different person now, and she hoped the change meant growth.

She glanced at the man in the seat beside her. Handsome. Distinguished. Her husband. His gray head was bent in concentration as he pored over reports on the economy and the stock market for the first time in days. He looked like a typical husband, settled into a routine of reading the morning paper. *Routine!* Lisle shivered. Was this the way her life would be now? Routine?

What in hell had she done? What would happen to the independence she had fought for so long and hard? Did it have to go out the window when she said "*Sí,* I do"? She knew it was too late to reconsider her decision. The ways of love dictate that the woman should be willing to change her life for the man she loves. Admittedly, she loved Hal. So why wasn't she going into his world willingly?

Their last night in Mexico, as she lay in Hal's strong arms, she had felt positive that she had done the right thing. Now, in reflection, she wasn't so sure. She had flown to Cancun as a woman of independent means. She was returning to Dallas as a married woman. Mrs. Hal Kammerman.

"What are you thinking, Lisle?"

She sighed, and the words just slipped out: "You really don't want to know."

"Having second thoughts?" Hal folded the newspaper and stuffed it into the pocket of the seat in front of him. Would regular husbands have folded the paper so quickly to talk to their wives? Was Hal a regular husband? Was she—it hurt to say—a regular wife?

Lisle looked up, alarmed that her husband could read her thoughts. Were they written so clearly on her face? Did he know her that well? "No second thoughts, Hal. Of course not," she denied, hoping her eyes didn't betray her.

"Regrets?"

"Not about our love." She slipped her hand into his, seeking the reassurance his touch always gave her. *It will be all right,* she repeated silently, trying to push aside the questions that nagged at her.

He brought her hand to his lips and let them play gently along her knuckles. "You know, love, things could have been very different for us if your assignment in Cancun hadn't been canceled back in February."

She grinned. "Not really. The deciding factor would have tipped us in the direction of marriage anyway."

"The deciding factor? You mean our love?"

She smiled wickedly. "When you sold your house in Wilmington, I knew I had to marry you, Hal. I couldn't have the man I love turned out on the streets!"

"Thanks," he said drolly. "But I would have managed somehow."

"I know," she admitted with a teasing smile. "I kept thinking of all those widows just waiting to take you in!"

"Rich, beautiful widows," he amended teasingly.

"I don't doubt it. And I was green with envy at the thought. You know I couldn't let anyone else have you, Hal. I love you too much. Anyway, nothing could be more romantic than being married in a Mexican ceremony and barely understanding the language!"

"If you want out, you can always claim you didn't understand what you were saying. *No comprende!*"

"Oh, I knew what I was saying. *Sí* to everything! Yes to you and to our love!" Lisle was trying desperately to believe this marriage was right for her. Did other women go through this torment, even after they had married the man they loved dearly with all their heart? Why was she even questioning it?

"You have made me an extremely happy man, Lisle." He kissed her palm.

"I'm happy too, Hal. Now, I can tell Image International to take a flying leap into the nearest ocean."

"Is that what you want to do?"

She smiled vindictively. "I've wanted to tell the boss to shove it so many times! Surely you know that."

"You've made such strides for the older woman in the modeling industry, I'd hate to see you give it up, just because of our marriage."

"Oh, I wouldn't. But the fact is, my career has already reached its peak. My assignments have been fewer lately, and my agent complains that it's harder to place me."

Hal grew thoughtful. "You know, Lisle, one way for you to gain control over the injustice of age discrimination is through power."

"Yes. And how do I get that power?"

"If you're the boss."

"Me? But I'm not in a position to be boss."

"You could be."

"How? You mean try starting my own agency? I don't have the money." She was still thinking very independently.

"Perhaps not by yourself, but I do have the money and I'm your husband. Stop thinking in such limited terms, Lisle. What's mine is yours. We could pool our resources. You have the inside knowledge of the business of modeling. I have the money and management skills to run it." He said it all very matter-of-factly, as one would expect of a man who was accustomed to making quick assessments of a situation.

Lisle was thunderstruck at the prospect! "Do you think it's possible? Is it really feasible? Would it work? Could we try it, Hal?"

"Of course! We'd make it work!" he said firmly. "It's just like our marriage, we have to work at it, Lisle. I'm willing to make some changes in my life-style, even my business, if you are. I'm ready to take the risks with you."

"What kind of risks are you talking about, Hal?" She felt that he was thinking way ahead of her.

Hal spoke unemotionally as he discussed certain practical considerations. "We could change the emphasis of the consulting firm. It wouldn't be too difficult for me to direct my energies to a new project."

"You'd let your business go, just like that? You'd really do it, Hal? I can't believe it!" Lisle was amazed at his coolness.

"I've told you I'm always ready for a new challenge, especially if it looks like a profitable endeavor. Having our own modeling agency sounds very exciting to me. I'd risk anything for you, Lisle. I want to start a new life with you, Lisle. We'll have a completely new life-style, even a new business."

"An agency?" She mouthed the words as if trying to digest the idea. "Our own agency? Oh, God, Hal, what a challenge! I'm getting excited, just thinking about it! My own models! Kammerman Agency—"

"No. Wheaton Agency," he told her firmly. "You have the recognizable name in the business, darling. There's only one condition for this Wheaton-Kammerman alliance. Neutral ground for both of us. We each start with even risks, including the location of the agency. Definitely not in Wilmington. Nor in Dallas. You'd be competing too closely with Image International."

Neutral ground? They would have to struggle like hell to

make it work. Equally. Each one dependent on the other for making it work. Each one independent of the other in accepting the risks involved. Lisle nodded enthusiastically. This was a risk she could live with and work to overcome, with Hal by her side.

"Where? Houston?" she suggested, thinking aloud.

"Too conservative for the type of models we'll be featuring." He shook his head.

"L.A.?"

"Too much competition from Hollywood glamour."

She paused to think, then said, "What about the center of fashion, New York?"

He pursed his lips. "Maybe. Yes, New York might be right. Could you live in New York? What do you think?"

"I think *sí, mi amor!* Yes to everything!" Lisle smiled happily and leaned over to kiss her husband with renewed love and admiration. They had a new purpose to their life together, new goals to seek. They would be making their own world.

"Hal, where are you? Are you ready?" Lisle called up the stairs of her Dallas town house.

"Up here," he answered from the tiny spare room he had turned into a makeshift office in the two days they had been in Dallas. "Come on up for a minute."

As she climbed the stairs Lisle explained, "The children and grandchildren will be here in fifteen minutes. I told you about our Sunday suppers. Sometimes it's a real zoo around here. Tonight you're to become an instant grandpa! You'll love the babies. Craig's daughter is Victoria. She's two and absolutely precious! She's just starting to say a few words. And then there's Alex, Inga's son. He will talk your ears off! He's positively delightful and very smart."

"I'm sure I'll get along fine with the little ones, but I thought tonight would be a wedding celebration for us."

She nodded and grinned. "Uh-huh. A wedding celebra-

186

tion for the grandparents. I think my family has hopes I'll settle down to being a real grandma, like I should."

"A real grandma? What's that?"

"Damned if I know!" She grinned impishly.

He ran his hand over the back of his head. "Grandpa, huh? And you're Grandma Wheaton?"

"Are you kidding?" She propped her hands on her slender hips. "I've always been Lisle to them!"

"Those little tykes call you Lisle?"

"You bet! Can you see me being called granny? I'm a new bride!" She bent to kiss him, and he caught her around the neck.

"Then you don't want to find yourself suddenly married to a grandpa. I guess I'll be Hal to them."

"Why not? It's your name! They'll understand. They're used to an offbeat grandmother. Why not the same kind of grandpa?"

"Do they know about the Viking?"

"No." She kissed him merrily. "That's our secret. I realize this is quite an adjustment for you, Hal. Instant adult children and toddler grandchildren come with this marriage, but I tried to warn you!"

He pursed his lips. "Oh, I figure I'll have adapted to them by the time you're reconciled to our marriage."

"Hal, darling, I'm perfectly happy in our married state."

"And I intend to keep you that way, my love, no matter what it takes."

"Right now it takes going downstairs to greet your new family."

"Wait a minute." Hal gestured to the paper before him. "I've been working on an organization chart for our new agency. Before the gang arrives, take a look. What do you think?"

She caught her breath and glanced quickly at the sheet of paper beneath his fingers. Was Hal taking charge already? He certainly had more organizational skills than she. Would that be a problem for them? The first words that caught her eyes were "Wheaton Agency" in large block letters. Her quivering finger followed the linked rectangles of job titles that branched out like a family tree.

CHAIRMAN of the BOARD—Lisle Wheaton
CHIEF EXECUTIVE OFFICER—Lisle Wheaton

Under her name a box linked to the others with a single line read

MANAGER—Hal Kammerman

"Now," he continued in his matter-of-fact business voice, "you can see I answer directly to you, Lisle. I prefer it that way, but if you have other ideas, we can discuss them, and make changes if necessary. I don't know which name you want to use. I would suggest Wheaton for business."

"And you can be called my wonderful Viking privately?" She wrapped her arms about his neck and scooted into his lap.

"Lisle, seriously now, what do you think?"

"I think I love you!"

"I mean about the chart."

She buried her face in his neck. "I love that too. How is it that you know just the right things to do to make me happy?"

"I know you, m'lady. And I know what it'll take to make you happy. Independence first. This agency is your baby. Believe me, you're going to have your share of problems as the boss. I'm only here to help you make managerial decisions. But the risk, Lisle, is ours to share."

"And I was afraid we would settle into a married life that was dull and routine."

"Dull and routine? Never!" Hal pulled Lisle firmly against his chest and kissed her. "Our love has never been dull. And

188

I don't intend for that to start now. Incidentally, my firm has a couple of contracts to be fulfilled before we call it quits. One is with a plastics company in Buffalo. The other is with an import company in Singapore.

"Now, I could send Ned McPherson, my chief executive officer, to complete both assignments. Or . . . you and I could go, do a little business, and have a honeymoon in the Far East. That is, unless you'd prefer to go to Buffalo."

"You're asking me? Foolish man! You know the answer to that already! Ship poor Ned off to Buffalo. We'll take care of the Far East!"

"You know, this will probably delay the opening of our agency by a couple of months."

"I don't care! Singapore sounds wonderful! It's so exotic! I've never ridden in a rickshaw, Hal!"

"You'll love Singapore, Lisle. It's a real fantasy land. There's ancient Chinese art, and all the Chinese food you can eat, and ballet troupes dancing in the streets. You'll be beautiful in a silk kimono and a jade necklace." He kissed the pulse point on her neck. "How would you like to make love in a Chinese junk?"

"Those little ships with the funny sails? You'll be my Genghis Khan, adventurer *extraordinaire!* I'd love it! And I love you!"

"I'll try to play the barbarian and somehow keep a balance between fantasy and reality."

"And love."

"And plenty of love . . ." His kiss grew deeper and lasted until the doorbell's rude intrusion.

"It's the children," Lisle announced, her hands immediately straightening her silk blouse. "And the grandchildren!"

"Can't you get rid of them?" Hal mumbled, trying to pull her close again.

"No! Come on, Hal!"

189

"Damn! Do we have to go away from home in order to make love whenever we want to?"

"Looks that way." She smiled and took his hand, knowing their fantasies, and their love, would continue. For a lifetime.

Now you can reserve May's Candlelights <u>before</u> they're published!

♥ You'll have copies set aside for *you* the instant they come off press.

♥ You'll save yourself precious shopping time by arranging for *home delivery.*

♥ You'll feel proud and efficient about organizing a system that *guarantees* delivery.

♥ You'll avoid the disappointment of not finding *every* title you want and need.

ECSTASY SUPREMES $2.50 each

☐ **REACH FOR THE SKY,** Barbara Andrews.................17242-X-11
☐ **LOTUS BLOSSOM,** Hayton Monteith.........................14907-X-22
☐ **PRIZED POSSESSION,** Linda Vail............................17116-4-30
☐ **HIGH VOLTAGE,** Lori Copeland 13604-0-12

ECSTASY ROMANCES $1.95 each

☐ **A GLIMPSE OF PARADISE,** Cathie Linz....................12857-9-26
☐ **WITH EACH CARESS,** Anne Silverlock.....................19730-9-16
☐ **JUST A KISS AWAY,** JoAnna Brandon.......................14402-7-14
☐ **WHEN MIDNIGHT COMES,** Edith Delatush..............19433-4-16
☐ **MORE THAN A DREAM,** Lynn Patrick 15828-1-17
☐ **HOLD CLOSE THE MEMORY,** Heather Graham 13696-2-11
☐ **A VISION OF LOVE,** Melanie Catley...........................18483-5-17
☐ **DIAMOND IN THE ROUGH,** Joan Grove 11892-1-33